The Three Investigators
in
The Secret of Terror Castle

Alfred Hitchcock
and
The Three Investigators
in

The Secret
of Terror Castle

Text by Robert Arthur
Illustrated by Harry Kane

Random House, New York

Contents

NOTICE TO THE READER: You are under no obligation whatever to read a single word of this introduction.

ALFRED J. HITCHCOCK

Introduction

I SEEM TO BE constantly introducing something. For years I've been introducing my television programs. I've introduced motion pictures. And I've introduced books of mystery, ghost and suspense stories for my fans to shiver with.

Now I find myself introducing a trio of lads who call themselves The Three Investigators, and ride around in a gold-plated Rolls-Royce, solving mysteries, riddles, enigmas and conundrums of all kinds. Preposterous, isn't it?

Frankly I would prefer to have nothing to do with these three youths, but I rashly promised to introduce them. And I am a man of my word—even though the promise was extorted from me by nothing less than sheer skulduggery, as you will see.

To the business at hand, then. The three boys who call themselves The Three Investigators are Bob Andrews, Pete Crenshaw, and Jupiter Jones, all of whom live in Rocky Beach, a small city on the shore of the Pacific Ocean some miles from Hollywood.

Bob Andrews, who is small but wiry, is something of a scholarly type, although with an adventurous spirit. Pete Crenshaw is quite tall and muscular. Jupiter Jones is—— Well, I shall refrain from giving you my own personal opinion of Jupiter Jones. You will have to decide about him for yourself after reading the pages that follow. I shall simply stick to the facts.

Therefore, though I would be sorely tempted to call Jupiter Jones fat, I will simply say, as his friends do, that he is stocky. As a very small child, Jupiter Jones appeared in a television series about a group of comical children—a series I am happy to say I never encountered. However, it appears that as an infant he was so fat and comical in appearance, he was known as Baby Fatso and made millions laugh at the way he kept falling over things.

This gave him a deep aversion to being laughed at. In order to get himself taken seriously, he studied furiously. From the time he could read, he read everything he could get his hands on—science, psychology, criminology, and many other subjects. Having a good memory, he retained much of what he read, so that in school his teachers found it best to avoid getting into arguments with him about questions of fact. They found themselves proved wrong too often.

If at this point Jupiter Jones sounds rather insufferable, I can only agree with you heartily. However, I am told he has many loyal friends. But then, there is no accounting for the tastes of the young.

Now I could tell you a great deal more about him and the other boys. I could tell you how Jupiter won the use of the gold-plated car in a contest. I could tell you how he established a local reputation for finding lost articles, including runaway pets. I could—— But I feel I have done my duty. I have more than lived up to my promise. If you haven't skipped all this long ago, you are probably even gladder than I am that this introduction is ended.

ALFRED HITCHCOCK

The Three Investigators
in
The Secret of Terror Castle

Chapter 1

The Three Investigators

BOB ANDREWS PARKED his bike outside his home in Rocky Beach and entered the house. As he closed the door, his mother called to him from the kitchen.

"Robert? Is that you?"

"Yes, Mom." He went to the kitchen door. His mother, brown-haired and slender, was making doughnuts.

"How was the library?" she asked.

"It was okay," Bob told her. After all, there was never any excitement at the library. He worked there part time, sorting returned books and helping with the filing and cataloguing.

"Your friend Jupiter called." His mother went on rolling out the dough on a board. "He left a message for you."

"A message?" Bob yelled with sudden excitement. "What was it?"

"I wrote it down. I'll get it out of my pocket as soon as I finish with this dough."

"Can't you remember what he said? He may need me!"

"I could remember an ordinary message," his mother answered, "but Jupiter doesn't leave ordinary messages. It was something fantastic."

"Jupiter likes unusual words," Bob said, controlling his impatience. "He's read an awful lot of books and sometimes he's a little hard to understand."

"Not just sometimes!" his mother retorted. "He's a very unusual boy. My goodness, how he found my engagement ring, I'll never know."

She was referring to the time the previous fall when she had lost her diamond ring. Jupiter Jones had come to the house and requested her to tell him every move she had made the day the ring was lost. Then he had gone out to the pantry, reached up, and picked the ring from behind a row of bottled tomato pickles. Bob's mother had taken it off and put it there while she was sterilizing the jars.

"I can't imagine," Mrs. Andrews said, "how he guessed where that ring was!"

"He didn't guess, he figured it out," Bob explained. "That's how his mind works. . . . Mom, can't you get the message now?"

"In one minute," his mother said, giving the dough another flattening roll.

"Incidentally, what on earth was that story on the front of yesterday's paper about Jupiter's winning the use of a Rolls-Royce sedan for thirty days?"

"It was a contest the Rent-'n-Ride Auto Rental Company had," Bob told her. "They put a big jar full of beans in their window and offered the Rolls-Royce and a chauffeur for thirty days to whoever guessed nearest to the right number of beans. Jupiter spent about three days calculating how much space was in the jar, and how many beans it would take to fill that space. And he won. . . . Mom, please, can't you find the message now?"

"All right," his mother agreed. She began to wipe the flour from her hands. "But what on earth will Jupiter Jones do with a Rolls-Royce sedan and a chauffeur, even for thirty days?"

"Well, you see, we're thinking——" Bob began, but by then his mother wasn't listening.

"These days a person can win almost anything," she was saying. "Why, I read about a woman who won a houseboat on a television program. She lives up in the mountains, and she's almost frantic, not knowing what to do with it." While she was talking, Mrs. Andrews had taken a slip of paper from her pocket.

"Here's the message," she said. "It says 'Green Gate One. The presses are rolling.' "

"Gosh, Mom, thanks," Bob yelled, and was almost out the front door before her voice stopped him.

"Robert, what on earth does the message mean? Is Jupiter using some kind of fantastic code?"

"No, Mom. It's plain, ordinary English. Well, I've got to hurry."

Bob popped out the door, swung onto his bike, and started for The Jones Salvage Yard.

When he was riding a bicycle, the brace on his leg bothered him scarcely at all. He had "won the brace," as Dr. Alvarez put it, by foolishly trying to climb one of the hills near Rocky Beach all alone. Rocky Beach is built on a flat spot, with the Pacific Ocean on one side and the Santa Monica Mountains on the other.

As mountains, they might be considered a bit small, but as hills they are very big. Bob had rolled down some five hundred feet of slope and wound up with his leg broken in umpteen places. A new record, the hospital assured him. However, Dr. Alvarez said that eventually the brace could come off and he would never know he had once worn it. Although it was sometimes a nuisance, it didn't really bother him most of the time.

Getting outside the main section of town, Bob reached The Jones Salvage Yard. It had been called Jones's Junkyard until Jupiter persuaded his uncle to change the name. Now it handled many unusual items in addition to ordinary junk, so that people came from miles away when they needed something they couldn't find elsewhere.

The yard was a fascinating spot for any boy, and its unusual character was obvious from as far away as one could see the board fence that surrounded it. Mr. Titus Jones had used a number of different colors of paint, acquired as junk, to paint the fence. Some of the local artists had helped him, because Mr. Jones was always letting them have some little piece of junk they needed, free.

The whole front section was covered with trees and flowers and green lakes and swans, and even an ocean scene. The other sides had other pictures. It was probably the most colorful junkyard in the country.

Bob rode past the front gate, which consisted of two enormous iron gates from an estate that had burned down. He went on almost a hundred yards farther and stopped near the corner, where the fence showed a green ocean with a two-masted sailing ship foundering in a raging storm. Bob dismounted and found the two green boards Jupe had made into a private gate. That was Green Gate One. He pushed against the eye of a fish that was looking out of the water at the sinking ship, and the boards swung up.

He shoved his bike through and closed the gate. Now he was inside the junkyard, in the corner which Jupiter had arranged as his outdoor workshop. It was outdoors except for a roof about six feet wide that ran around most of the fence on the inside of the yard. Mr. Jones kept his better junk under this roof.

As Bob entered the workshop, Jupiter Jones was sitting in an old swivel chair, pinching his lower lip, always a sign that his mental machinery was spinning in high gear. Pete Crenshaw was busy at the small printing press which had come in as junk, and which Jupiter had labored over until it would operate again.

The printing press was going *clink-clank,* back and

forth. Tall, dark-haired Pete was busy putting down and picking up white cards. That was what Jupe's message had meant—simply that the press was working and he wanted Bob to come meet them through Green Gate One.

No one could see the boys from the main part of the junkyard where the office was—especially Jupiter's Aunt Mathilda, a large woman, who really ran the business. She had a big heart, and was endlessly good-natured, but when she saw a boy around she had only one idea: Put him to work!

In self-defense Jupiter had, bit by bit, arranged the piles of various types of junk in the yard so they hid his workshop from sight. Now he and his friends could have privacy when he was not actually needed to help his uncle or his aunt.

As Bob parked his bike, Pete shut off the press and handed him one of the cards he had been printing.

"Look at that!" he said.

It was a large business card. And it said:

THE THREE INVESTIGATORS
"We Investigate Anything"
? ? ?

First Investigator   — Jupiter Jones
Second Investigator   — Peter Crenshaw
Records and Research — Bob Andrews

"Golly!" Bob said admiringly. "That really has zing. So you decided to go ahead with it, Jupe?"

"We've been talking for a long time about starting an investigation agency," Jupiter said. "And now my winning the use of a Rolls-Royce sedan for thirty days of twenty-four hours each gives us freedom to seek mystery wherever we may find it. For a certain time, anyway. Therefore we are taking the plunge. We are now officially The Three Investigators.

"As First Investigator, I will be in charge of planning. As Second Investigator, Pete will be in charge of all operations requiring athletic prowess. As you are at present somewhat handicapped in shadowing suspects or climbing fences, and similar duties, Bob, you will handle all of the research our cases may need. You will also keep complete records of everything we do."

"That's fine with me," Bob said. "With my library job it will be easy for me to do research."

"Modern investigation requires extensive research," Jupiter said. "But you are staring at our business card in an odd manner. May I ask what is troubling you?"

"Well, it's these question marks," Bob said. "What are they for?"

"I was waiting for you to ask that," Pete said. "Jupe said you would. He says everyone will."

"The question mark," Jupiter said impressively, "is the universal symbol of something unknown. We are prepared to solve any puzzle, riddle, mystery, enigma or conundrum which may be brought to us. Hence the question mark will be our trademark. Three question marks together will always stand for The Three Investigators."

Bob thought Jupiter was finished, but he should have known better. Jupiter was just warming up.

"In addition," Jupiter said, "the question marks will provoke interest. They will make people ask us what they mean, just as you did. They will help people remember us. They will be good publicity. Every business needs publicity in order to attract potential customers."

"That's great," Bob said, putting the card back on the pile Pete had already printed. "Now we'd be in business if we only had a case to investigate."

Pete looked important.

"Bob," he said, "we've got a case!"

"Correction," Jupiter said. He straightened up and set his jaw. When he did so, his face, normally rather round, seemed longer and he looked older. Stockily built, Jupiter could look a little fat when he did not hold himself erect.

"Unfortunately," Jupiter explained, "one small obstacle remains. There is a case available for us—one I feel we can easily solve—but we have not yet been engaged."

"What is the case?" Bob asked eagerly.

"Mr. Alfred Hitchcock is looking for a real haunted house for his next picture," Pete said. "Dad heard about it at the studio." Mr. Crenshaw was a special-effects man who worked at one of the movie studios in Hollywood, a few miles away across the hills.

"A haunted house?" Bob frowned. "How can you solve a haunted house?"

"We can investigate the haunted house and find out if it is really haunted or not. The publicity will get our name known and The Three Investigators will be launched."

"Only Mr. Hitchcock hasn't asked us to investigate any haunted houses for him," Bob said. "Is that what you call a small obstacle?"

"We shall have to persuade him to engage our services," Jupiter said. "That's the next step."

"Sure," Bob said with rich sarcasm. "I suppose we are going to march into the office of one of the most famous movie producers in the world and say, 'You sent for us, sir?' "

"The details are not quite correct but the idea is roughly accurate," Jupiter told him. "I have already telephoned Mr. Hitchcock for an appointment."

"You have?" Pete asked, looking as surprised as Bob. "And he said he'd see us?"

"No," the stocky boy admitted. "His secretary wouldn't even let me talk to him."

"That figures," Pete said.

"In fact, she said she would have us arrested if we came anywhere near him," Jupiter added. "It turns out that Mr. Hitchcock's temporary secretary this summer is a girl who used to go to school here in Rocky Beach. She was a number of grades ahead of us but you should remember her. Henrietta Larson."

"Bossy Henrietta!" Pete exclaimed. "You bet I remember her."

"She used to help the teachers and boss all the little kids around," Bob added. "Do I remember! If Henrietta Larson is Mr. Hitchcock's secretary, we'd better forget it. Three tigers couldn't get past her."

"Obstacles," Jupiter replied, "are what make life interesting. Tomorrow morning we will all drive to Hollywood and call on Mr. Hitchcock in our new temporary car."

"And have Henrietta sic the police on us?" Bob yelled. "Besides, I have to work at the library all day tomorrow."

"Then Pete and I will go. I will phone the Rent-'n-Ride Auto Rental Agency and tell them I shall start my use of the car at ten o'clock tomorrow morning. And you, Bob," Jupiter went on, "as long as you are going to be at the library tomorrow, look in the old newspaper and magazine files for information about this."

He wrote two words—*Terror Castle*—on back of one of the business cards and handed it to Bob. The other boy read it and gulped.

"All right, Jupe," he said. "If you say so."

"The Three Investigators are now in business," Jupiter announced, looking satisfied. "Carry a supply of our cards with you at all times. They will be your credentials. And tomorrow every man will do his duty, come what may."

Chapter 2

A Fateful Interview

WELL BEFORE THE Rolls-Royce was due to arrive at The Jones Salvage Yard the following morning, Pete and Jupiter were standing outside the big iron gates, waiting. They both wore their Sunday suits, with white shirts and neckties. Their hair was plastered into place and their faces glowed pink through their normal tan. Even their fingernails glowed from the application of a stiff brush.

But when at last the big car arrived, its gleam far outshone theirs. It was a Rolls-Royce of rather ancient vintage, with huge headlights like snare drums and a tremendously long hood. The body was square and boxlike. But all the trimming—even the bumpers—was gold-plated, and it gleamed like jewelry. The black body shone with such a deep luster it was almost a mirror.

"Golly," Pete said reverently as the car came toward them. "It looks like a car a billionaire a hundred and ten years old would ride in."

"The Rolls-Royce is the most expensive regular

production model car in the world," Jupiter said. "This one was originally built for a rich Arabian sheik of luxurious tastes. Now the company uses it mostly for publicity purposes."

The car came to a stop, and the chauffeur whipped out of the front seat. He was a lean, powerfully built man more than six feet tall, with a long, good-humored face. He removed his chauffeur's cap and addressed Jupiter.

"Master Jones?" he said. "I am Worthington, the chauffeur."

"Uh—glad to meet you, Mr. Worthington," Jupiter said. "But call me Jupiter, like everybody else."

"Please, sir." Worthington looked pained. "You must address me simply as Worthington. That is customary. It is also customary for me to address my employers in a somewhat formal manner. You are now my employer, as it were, and I would prefer to adhere to custom."

"Well, all right, Worthington," Jupiter said. "If it's customary."

"Thank you, sir. Now the car and I are at your service for thirty days."

"Thirty days of twenty-four hours each," Jupiter said. "That's how the contest rules were worded."

"Precisely, sir." Worthington opened the rear door. "Will you enter?"

"Thank you," Jupiter said, as he and his partner clambered in. "But you don't have to open doors for us. We're young enough to do that for ourselves."

"If you don't mind, sir," Worthington answered, "I would prefer to render every service I'm supposed to. If I don't, I might get slack in the future."

"I see." Jupiter mulled that over as Worthington took his place behind the wheel. "But we may want to get in or out in a hurry sometimes, Worthington. We might not be able to wait for you. Suppose we get in and out by ourselves, except at the beginning and ending of a trip."

"Very good, sir." In the rear-view mirror they could see the British chauffeur smiling. "A very neat solution."

"Uh—we probably won't be as dignified as most of the people you've driven around," Jupiter confided. "And we may want to go to some unusual spots. . . . This will help explain."

He handed one of The Three Investigators' business cards to Worthington, who studied it gravely.

"I believe I understand, sir," Worthington said. "I am quite looking forward to this assignment. It will be a change to drive someone young and adventurous. Most of my passengers recently have been rather elderly and cautious. Now our first destination, sir?"

Pete and Jupiter found themselves taking a great liking to the chauffeur.

"We want to go to World Studios, in Hollywood, to call on Mr. Alfred Hitchcock," Jupiter said. "I—uh— I telephoned him yesterday."

"Very good, Master Jones."

A moment later the luxurious car was purring up the road that led over the hills toward Hollywood. Worthington spoke over his shoulder. "I should inform you that this car has a telephone and a refreshment compartment, both of which are at your service."

"Thank you," Jupiter said, already acting dignified, as befitted the occupant of such a car. Reaching in front of him, he opened a compartment and lifted out a telephone. Like the trimming on the car, it was gold-plated. It had no dial, however—just a button to be pushed.

"A mobile telephone," he informed Pete. "One pushes the button and gives the desired number to the operator. I don't think we have any need for it just yet, however." Somewhat reluctantly Jupiter put the phone away again and settled back against the leather upholstery.

The drive was pleasant but uneventful, and soon they were riding through the business section of Hollywood. As they drew nearer their destination, Pete began to squirm uneasily on the seat.

"Jupe," he said, "I wish you'd tell me how we're ever going to get through the studio gate. You know perfectly well all studios have walls and gatemen just to keep out people like us. We'll never get inside."

"I have a strategy in mind," Jupiter said. "I only hope it will work, for we seem to have arrived."

They were driving past high stucco walls that extended for a full two blocks. A sign on top said WORLD STUDIOS. The wall was there for just one reason—to keep people out, as Pete had said.

In the center was a tall iron gate that stood open. A man in uniform sat in a small cubbyhole beside it. Worthington swung the Rolls into the driveway, and the guard jumped up. "Hey, wait a minute!" he yelled. "Where're you going?"

Worthington stopped the car.

"We are calling on Mr. Alfred Hitchcock."

"You have a pass?" the guard asked.

"We did not expect to need a pass," Worthington replied. "The master telephoned Mr. Hitchcock."

Which was perfectly true, of course. Even if Mr. Hitchcock hadn't answered.

"Oh." The guard scratched his head uncertainly. Jupiter lowered the window on his side and leaned out.

"My good man," he said, and Pete almost jumped, because Jupe was speaking in a rich, English accent he had never used before but must have practiced in secret. "My good man, what seems to be the delay?"

"Gleeps!" Pete whispered to himself. He knew that Jupe had been an actor in television when he was just a tiny kid, and he had a real talent for impersonations, but Pete had never seen him do this one before.

By puffing out his cheeks and lips a bit and looking down his nose, Jupe had turned into a dead ringer for

Alfred Hitchcock himself! A rather impertinent young Alfred Hitchcock, of course, but nobody could miss the resemblance.

"Uh—I have to know who's calling on Mr. Hitchcock," the guard said nervously.

"I see." Jupiter gave him another down-the-nose look. "Perhaps I had better phone my uncle."

He took out the gold-plated telephone, pressed the button and asked for a number. It was the number of The Jones Salvage Yard. Jupiter was really calling his uncle.

The guard took one more look at the amazing car and at Jupiter Jones using the gold telephone.

"Uh, you just go on in," the guard said hurriedly. "I'll phone you're on your way."

"Thank you," Jupiter said. "Drive on, Worthington."

The car moved on. Jupiter settled back as they turned down a narrow street bordered on both sides by green lawns and palm trees, with dozens of small, attractive bungalows set close together among them. Farther on were the arched roofs of the big studios where movies and television films were made. Actors in costume were filing toward one of them.

Although the car was now inside the studio, Pete still couldn't figure how even his partner could get in to see Mr. Hitchcock. But he had little time to worry, for Worthington was already pulling up beside a large bungalow. As was customary in many studios, each

producer had a bungalow of his own where he could work without being disturbed. A neatly painted sign said: ALFRED HITCHCOCK.

"Wait for us, Worthington," Jupiter said, as the chauffeur opened the door. "I don't know how long we will be."

"Very good, sir."

Jupe led the way up the one step, and through the screen door into the air-cooled reception room. A blonde girl behind a desk was just putting down the phone. Pete had trouble recognizing the grown-up Henrietta Larson, but as soon as she spoke he knew her.

"So!" Henrietta put her hands on her hips and looked at Jupiter Jones. "You're here, are you? Impersonating Mr. Hitchcock's nephew! Well, now we'll see just how long it takes the studio police to get rid of you."

Pete's heart sank to his socks as she reached for the telephone again. "Wait!" Jupiter said.

"Wait for what?" Henrietta Larson asked scornfully. "You got in here by telling the guard at the gate you're Mr. Hitchcock's nephew——"

"No, he didn't." Pete defended his partner. "The guard just jumped to conclusions."

"You keep out of this," Henrietta warned Pete. "Jupiter Jones is a public nuisance and I'm going to see he's taken care of."

She bent over the telephone again. Jupiter spoke once more.

"It is never wise to act hastily, Miss Larson," he

said, and Pete jumped. Jupiter was using that rich English voice again, and in the space of a moment he had returned to the appearance which had so impressed the gateman—the appearance of a very youthful Alfred Hitchcock.

"I feel sure Mr. Hitchcock would be interested in seeing this display of my acting talents," Jupiter finished. Henrietta Larson, looking up, dropped the telephone as if it had stung her.

"Why, you——" she began. "You——" For a moment words seemed to fail her. Then her face became grim. "Yes, indeed, Jupiter Jones, I'm positive Mr. Hitchcock will want to see this display."

"Ahem. . . . Miss Larson."

Both boys hastily turned around at the unexpected sound of a voice behind them. Even Henrietta appeared startled. There in the office door stood Alfred Hitchcock himself.

"Is there something wrong, Miss Larson?" Mr. Hitchcock asked. "I've been ringing for you."

"It's for you to decide if there is anything wrong, Mr. Hitchcock," Henrietta Larson said. "This young man has something to show you in which I am sure you will be very interested."

"I'm sorry," Mr. Hitchcock said. "I can't see anyone today. Send him away."

"I'm positive you'll want to see this, Mr. Hitchcock," Henrietta Larson said, and there was a tone in her voice Pete did not like at all. Mr. Hitchcock caught it, too, for he looked quizzically at the two boys, then shrugged.

"Very well. Follow me, lads."

He turned and strode to a desk the size of a tennis court. There he sat down in a swivel chair. Jupiter and Pete stood facing him as Henrietta shut the door.

"Now, boys," Mr. Hitchcock said, "what is it that I am supposed to see? I can spare you only five minutes."

"This is what I wanted to show you, sir," Jupiter said respectfully and whipped out one of The Three Investigators' business cards. Pete realized that Jupiter was following some plan of strategy that he had previously concocted. Apparently it was working. Mr. Hitchcock took the card and studied it.

"Hmmm," he said. "So you are investigators. May I ask what the question marks are for? Do they indicate a doubt in your own ability?"

"No, sir," Jupiter answered. "They are our trademark. They are symbolical of questions to be answered, of mysteries to be solved. Also, they make people ask questions, and that helps them remember us."

"I see." Mr. Hitchcock gave a little cough. "You are publicity-minded."

"A business can't succeed if people don't know about it," Jupiter said.

"A statement which cannot be disputed," Mr. Hitchcock agreed. "But speaking of business, you have not yet stated yours."

"We want to find a haunted house for you, sir."

"A haunted house?" Alfred Hitchcock's eyebrows rose. "What makes you think I want a haunted house?"

"We understand you want to find an authentic haunted house to use in your next suspense picture, sir," Jupiter said. "The Three Investigators desire to assist you in the search."

Alfred Hitchcock chuckled.

"I have two location scouts searching for a proper house at this moment," he said. "One is in Salem, Massachusetts, and the other in Charleston, South Carolina. Both places are rich in supernatural lore. Tomorrow the two men will go to Boston and New Orleans. I'm sure they will find me the right house for my purposes."

"But if we could find you the right house here in California, it would be a lot simpler to make your picture here, sir," Jupiter argued.

"I am sorry, my lad, it is out of the question."

"We don't want any money, sir," Jupiter said. "But all famous detectives have someone write up their cases for people to read—Sherlock Holmes, Ellery Queen, Hercule Poirot, all of them. I have deduced that that is how they become famous. In order to get potential customers to know about The Three Investigators, we will have our cases written up by the father of our other partner, Bob Andrews. He works for a newspaper."

"Well?" Alfred Hitchcock looked at his watch.

"Well, Mr. Hitchcock, I thought if you could just introduce our first case——"

"Quite impossible. Please ask Miss Larson to come in on your way out."

"Yes, sir." Jupiter looked depressed as he and Pete turned toward the door. They had almost reached it when Alfred Hitchcock spoke.

"One moment, lads."

"Yes, sir?" They turned. Mr. Hitchcock was looking at them with a frown.

"It occurs to me that you have not been entirely frank. What exactly was it that Miss Larson thought I should see? Not your business card, I'm sure."

"Well, sir," Jupiter said reluctantly, "I can do various impersonations, and she thought you would want to see my impersonation of you as a boy."

"Impersonation of me as a boy?" The famous director's voice grew deeper. His features clouded. "Just what do you mean?"

"This, sir." And once again Jupiter's face seemed to change shape. His voice deepened and took on an English accent, and he became a different individual.

"It occurred to me, Mr. Hitchcock," he said, in a voice entirely different from his own, "that someday you might wish to have someone portray you as a boy in a motion picture, and if you did——"

Mr. Hitchcock's brow had wrinkled. His face was dark with displeasure.

"Monstrous!" he said. "Stop it at once!"

Jupiter resumed his own identity.

"You don't think it's a good likeness?" he asked. "I mean, of you when you were a boy?"

"Certainly not. In any case, I was a fine, upstanding lad, not at all like that gross caricature you just attempted."

"Then I guess I'll have to practice some more," Jupiter sighed. "My friends thought it was very good."

"I forbid it!" Alfred Hitchcock thundered. "I absolutely forbid it! Give me your promise never again to do that particular impersonation and I . . . confound it, I'll introduce whatever you write about your case."

"Thank you, Mr. Hitchcock!" Jupiter said. "Then you want us to investigate the haunted house situation for you?"

"Oh, yes, yes, I suppose so. I don't promise to use it even if you find it, but investigate by all means. Now get out of here before I lose my last vestige of self-control. I take a very dim view of lads such as you. You are entirely too clever for your own good, young man."

Jupiter and Pete raced out toward the car, leaving Alfred Hitchcock looking darkly thoughtful as they went.

Chapter 3

Report on Terror Castle

IT WAS RATHER LATE in the afternoon, and Bob Andrews was puffing as he pushed his bike up to Green Gate One. What a time to have a flat tire!

He rolled the bike inside the salvage yard and parked it. Over in the main part of the yard he could hear the voice of Mrs. Jones, giving orders to Hans and Konrad, her husband's two helpers. But Jupiter and Pete were not in their workshop.

Bob had expected that. He went behind the little printing press and moved aside a section of old iron grating that seemed merely to be leaning against the bottom of a workbench. Behind the grating lay a very long, large galvanized pipe. He ducked into the open end of the pipe, pulled the grating back into place, then crawled as fast as his brace would let him through the pipe. This was "Tunnel Two," one of several secret entrances the boys could use to enter "Headquarters." It ended at a wooden panel. He pushed on the panel and it swung up. He was inside Headquarters.

Headquarters was a thirty-foot mobile home trailer that Titus Jones had bought for junk a year earlier. It had been badly damaged in a wreck, and he hadn't been able to sell it because of the great dents in the frame. So he had allowed Jupiter to use if for a kind of office.

In the course of the year, the three boys, with the help of Hans and Konrad, had gradually piled heaps of junk all around the outside of the trailer. Now, from the outside, it was entirely hidden by piles of steel bars, a section of a dilapidated fire escape, and some stacks of lumber and other material.

Mr. Jones had apparently forgotten all about its existence. And no one but the boys themselves knew that they had equipped the now well-hidden trailer as an office, laboratory and photographic darkroom, with several hidden entrances.

When Bob crawled out of the pipe, Jupiter was sitting in a rebuilt swivel chair behind a desk that had had one end scorched in a fire. (All the equipment in Headquarters had been rebuilt from junk.) Pete Crenshaw was sitting on the other side of the desk.

"You're late," Jupiter said as if Bob didn't know it.

"I had a flat tire." Bob was panting. "I ran over a big nail right outside the library."

"Did you find out anything?"

"I certainly did. I found out more than I want to know about Terror Castle."

"Terror Castle!" Pete exclaimed. "That's a name I don't like!"

"Wait until you hear about it," Bob told him. "About the family of five who tried to spend a night in it and were never——"

"Begin at the beginning," Jupiter requested. "Give us the facts in sequence."

"Okay." Bob started to open the large brown envelope he had brought with him. "But first I ought to tell you that Skinny Norris kept hanging over my shoulder all morning, trying to snoop into what I was doing."

"I hope you didn't let that goop know anything!" Pete exclaimed. "He's always trying to poke his nose into everything we're doing."

"I certainly didn't *tell* him anything. But he was awfully persistent. When I arrived at the library, he stopped me and wanted to talk about Jupe's winning the car for thirty days. He asked me how I thought he was going to use it."

"Skinny is just annoyed because he wants to be the only one in school who has his own car," Jupiter said. "If his father wasn't a legal resident of a state where they give out drivers' licenses practically to infants, Skinny wouldn't be able to drive any more than we can. Well, he can't lord it over us now."

"Anyway, while I was working in the library," Bob went on, frowning, "he kept watching me draw out all the old magazines and newspapers I needed to get the information for you, Jupe. I didn't let him get a look at what I was reading but——"

"Yes?" the First Investigator asked.

"You know our business card, on which you wrote 'Terror Castle' when you asked me to find out anything I could about the place?"

"I suppose you put it down while you were looking in the card catalogue, and couldn't find it again," Jupiter said.

Bob blinked. "How did you know?" he asked.

"You wouldn't have mentioned it if you hadn't lost it," Jupiter said. "And the most natural place to lose it would be in the library while you were examining the card catalogue."

"Well, that's what happened," Bob said. "I guess I must have left it on the table. I can't be sure Skinny Norris took it, but when he went away he was looking awfully pleased with himself."

"We can't concern ourselves with Skinny Norris now," Jupiter said. "We have an important case to proceed upon. Tell us what you learned."

"Sure." Bob took a number of papers from the envelope.

"To begin with," he said, "Terror Castle is located in a narrow little canyon up above Hollywood, called Black Canyon. It was originally called Terrill's Castle, because it was built by a movie actor named Stephen Terrill. He was a big star back in the silent-film days before talking pictures were invented.

"He used to play in all kinds of scary pictures about vampires and werewolves and stuff like that. He built his house to look like the haunted castle set used in one of his pictures, and filled it full of old suits of armor and Egyptian mummy cases and other weird things that came from the different pictures he'd acted in."

"Very promising," Jupiter said.

"That depends on what you're promising!" Pete yipped. "What became of this Stephen Terrill?"

"I'm coming to that," Bob said. "Stephen Terrill was known all over the world as 'The Man with a Million Faces.' Then talking pictures were invented. And people discovered he had a squeaky, high-pitched voice and lisped."

"Great!" Pete remarked. "A monster who lisped in a squeaky voice. They must have laughed themselves right off the seats."

"That's just what they did. And Stephen Terrill had to stop making pictures. He sent away all his servants, and then he sent away his best friend—his business manager, a Mr. Jonathan Rex. And finally he stopped answering the telephone or mail. He just shut himself up in his castle and brooded. People gradually began to forget about him.

"Then one day a wrecked car was discovered, about twenty-five miles north of Hollywood. It had run off the road and crashed down over the cliffs, almost into the ocean."

"Well, what did that have to do with Stephen Terrill?" Pete interrupted.

"The police traced the license number and learned that the car belonged to Terrill," Bob explained. "They didn't find his body, but that wasn't surprising. It would have washed away at high tide."

"Gee!" Pete looked serious. "Do you think he drove over the cliff on purpose?"

"They weren't sure," Bob answered. "But when the police went out to Black Canyon to look around the castle, the door was wide open. And there was nobody around. While they were searching the place, they found a note tacked to the library table. It said"—Bob checked his notes— " 'Though the world will never see me alive again, my spirit will never leave this place. The castle will be forevermore accursed.' And it was signed 'Stephen Terrill.' "

"Wow!" Pete exclaimed. "The more I hear about this place, the less I like it."

"On the contrary," Jupiter retorted, "it grows steadily more promising. Continue, Bob."

"Well, the police searched every nook and cranny of the old castle, but they never found any more trace of Terrill than the note. It turned out, though, that he owed the bank a lot of money—they had a mortgage on the place. They sent some men out to collect Stephen Terrill's possessions, but the men began to grow more and more nervous—they couldn't explain why—and they refused to finish the job. They did say they had heard and seen some very peculiar things, but they couldn't seem to describe them very clearly. Finally the bank tried to sell the castle just as it was, but they couldn't find anybody who would even live in it, much less buy it. Everybody who entered the place found themselves getting extremely nervous after a little while.

"One real estate agent went there to spend a whole night just to prove it was all imagination. He ran out at midnight, so frightened he ran all the way down the canyon."

Jupiter looked highly pleased. Pete gulped.

"Go on," Jupiter said. "This is better than I hoped for."

"Several other people tried to spend the night," Bob told them. "A movie starlet did it for the publicity. She ran out even before midnight, her teeth chattering so hard she could hardly talk. All she could do was whimper about a blue phantom and a fog of fear."

"A blue phantom and a fog of fear?" Pete licked his lips. "Nothing else, huh? No headless horsemen, no ghosts with clanking chains, no——"

"If you would let Bob finish," Jupiter interrupted, "we would be able to proceed faster."

"As far as I'm concerned," Pete muttered darkly, "he *is* finished. I don't care to hear any more."

Jupiter ignored this. "Anything else, Bob?"

"Well," Bob said, "just other incidents of the same kind. In one case a family of five from the East moved in—the bank offered them free rent for a year if they could break the jinx. But they were never heard from again. They just . . . well . . . disappeared the first night."

"Were there any manifestations?" Jupiter asked. "Sighs, moans, groans, ghostly shapes, and the like?"

"Not at first," Bob told him. "But later on there were plenty—distant groans, occasionally a misty figure walking up the stairs, and sometimes a sigh. Once in a while a muffled scream seemed to come from down underneath the castle. A lot of people reported having heard weird music coming from the ruined pipe organ in the music room. And several actually saw a ghostly figure, just a sort of shimmery blue blob, playing the organ. They named it the Blue Phantom."

"Surely these supernatural manifestations were investigated?"

"A couple of professors did move in to check up," Bob said, referring to his notes. "They didn't hear or see much. They just felt very uneasy the whole time. Worried. Upset. After they left, the bank decided it would never be able to sell the place, so it just closed off the road and let the castle sit there.

"For more than twenty years there's no record that anyone managed to spend a whole night there. One article said that at first bums and tramps tried to use it for a headquarters, but they couldn't stay there either. And they spread such stories about it that no tramp would go within a mile of the place.

"The last few years there aren't any stories about Terror Castle in the papers or magazines. As far as I could learn," Bob said, "Terror Castle is still just sitting there, vacant and deserted. The bank never could sell it, and no one ever goes near the place because there isn't any reason to."

"I'll say there isn't," Pete stated. "You couldn't hire me to go there."

"Nevertheless," Jupiter said, "we are going there—tonight. You and I will pay a preliminary visit to Terror Castle with camera and tape recorder, to see if it is still haunted. What we learn will give us a basis for a fuller investigation later. But I am most hopeful that we will find the place is genuinely haunted. If it is, it should be exactly right for Mr. Hitchcock's next picture."

Chapter 4

Into Terror Castle

BOB HAD A good deal more information in his notes about Terror Castle, and Jupiter read it all carefully. Pete kept saying wild horses couldn't drag him near the place, but when the time came to set out he was ready. Dressed in some old clothes, he was carrying the portable tape recorder he had gotten from a boy in school by trading his stamp collection for it.

Bob had a notebook and a couple of sharp pencils. Jupiter had his camera with the built-in flash bulb. Both Pete and Bob had told their families they were going driving with Jupiter in the car he had won for thirty days. Their parents seemed to feel that as long as Jupiter was with them everything would be fine. And then, of course, they knew that Worthington, the chauffeur, went with the car.

The big Rolls-Royce with the huge old headlights came easing up to The Jones Salvage Yard as soon as it was dark, and they piled in. Jupiter had a map showing the location of Black Canyon. Worthington looked at it, said, "Very good, Master Jones," and started off.

As they were rolling along through the hills, around all the twists and turns, Jupiter gave final instructions.

"This visit," he said, "is just to get a first impression. But if we see anything unusual, I'll take a flash-bulb picture of it. If we hear any sounds, you, Pete, capture them on your tape recorder."

"If I have to use this tape recorder," Pete said, as Worthington turned into a narrow road with steep hills on both sides, "all you'll hear will be the sound of chattering teeth."

"You, Bob," Jupiter continued, "will wait in the car for our return."

"That's the kind of job I like," Bob said. "Golly, but it's dark along here."

They were still climbing up a narrow, winding road. without a house in sight anywhere.

"Whoever named it Black Canyon knew what he was doing," Pete said.

"We seem to have reached an obstruction," Jupiter observed.

A mass of rocks and gravel blocked the road. The hills in that section of California, though sometimes covered thickly with mesquite and other bushes, had very little grass on them. So it was easy for rocks to roll down into the road. Here, a rock slide seemed to have knocked down some crossbars which might have been put up once, long before, to bar passage.

Worthington pulled the car off to one side.

"I fear we can proceed no farther," he reported. "But it is my impression from the map that the canyon should not extend more than a few hundred yards around that turn ahead."

"Thank you, Worthington. Come on, Pete, we will walk the rest of the way."

They climbed out.

"We'll be back in an hour!" Jupiter called to Worthington, who was carefully maneuvering the car to turn it around.

"Golly," Pete Crenshaw said, an apprehensive note in his voice, "that place looks scary."

Jupiter, crouched beside him in the darkness, said nothing. He was intently surveying the scene ahead. At the far end of the dark, narrow canyon the two boys could just make out the faint outlines of a fantastic structure. Against the starlit sky a round, peaked tower stood out clearly. But with the exception of the tower, Terror Castle was almost invisible. Placed as it was, at the head of the narrow, rock-strewn canyon and built high against one wall, the castle-like building was enveloped in murky shadow.

"I think we ought to come by daylight," Pete suddenly suggested. "So we can find our way around."

Jupiter shook his head.

"Nothing ever happens here in the daytime," he said. "It's only at night that this place scares people out of their wits."

"You're forgetting those men from the bank," Pete argued. "And besides, I don't want to be scared out of my wits. I'm halfway there already."

"So am I," Jupiter admitted. "I feel as if I had swallowed some butterflies."

"Then let's go back," Pete exclaimed with great relief. "We've done enough for one night. We ought to go back to Headquarters and make some more plans."

"I've already made my plans," his stocky companion said, and stood up. "My plans are to stay in Terror Castle for one hour tonight."

He started up the road, using a flashlight to pick his way around the rocks that had tumbled down from the steep canyon walls onto the cracked concrete. After a moment Pete hurried after him.

"If I'd known it was going to be like this," he complained, "I'd never have become an investigator."

"You'll feel better after we solve the mystery," Jupiter told him. "Think of what a wonderful start it will give our investigation firm."

"But suppose we meet the ghost? Or the Blue Phantom, or the mad spook, or whatever it is that haunts this place?"

"That's exactly what I want." Jupiter slapped the compact flash camera which hung from his shoulder. "If we can get its picture, we'll be famous."

"Suppose *it* gets *us?*" Pete retorted.

"S-s-sh!" his stocky friend said, stopping and snap-

ping off his flashlight. Pete froze into silence and the darkness closed around them.

Somebody—or *something*—was coming down the hillside directly toward them.

Pete crouched down. Beside him Jupe was swiftly getting his camera ready.

The noise, a pattering of rock displaced by moving feet, was almost on them when Jupe's flash bulb lit up the night. In the sudden radiance of the flash, Pete saw two huge red eyes leaping directly at him. Then something furry scurried past, struck the concrete road and went bounding away. In its wake several small rocks rolled down and came to rest at the boys' feet.

"A jack rabbit!" Jupiter said. He sounded disappointed. "We frightened it."

"We frightened *it!*" Pete exclaimed. "What do you think it did to *me?*"

"The natural effect of mysterious sound and movement at night upon a susceptible nervous system," Jupiter said. "Forward!" He grabbed Pete's arm and pulled him along. "We don't have to move quietly now —the flash bulb will have alerted the phantom, if there is a phantom."

"Can we sing?" Pete asked, reluctantly falling into step beside him. "If we sing 'Row, row, row your boat' loudly enough, we won't be able to hear the spook moan and groan."

"There's no need to go to extremes," the other boy said firmly. "We want to hear any moans and groans—

also any screams, sighs, screeches or rattling of chains, all of which are supposed to be common manifestations of a supernatural presence."

Pete suppressed the impulse to tell his partner that he had no desire whatever to hear any moans, groans, screams, screeches, sighs or rattling chains. He knew there was no point in it. When Jupiter made up his mind, he made up his mind. He was about as easy to move as a large rock.

As they moved forward the rambling old building loomed larger, gloomier, and altogether less desirable. Pete tried hard to forget all the stories Bob had told them about the old place.

After a last stretch along a high, crumbling stone wall, the two boys entered the main courtyard of Terror Castle.

"Here we are," Jupiter said, and stopped.

One tower stretched skyward far above them. Another, shorter tower seemed to scowl down at them. Blank windows were like blind eyes reflecting the starlight.

Suddenly something flew around their heads. Pete ducked.

"Wow," he yelled. "A bat!"

"Bats only eat insects," Jupiter reminded him. "They never eat people."

"Maybe this one wants a change of diet. Why take chances?"

Jupiter pointed to the wide doorway and the big, carved front door directly ahead.

"There is the door," he said. "Now all we have to do is walk through it."

"I wish I could get my legs to believe that. They think we ought to go back."

"So do mine," Jupiter admitted. "But my legs take orders from me. Come on."

He strode forward. Pete couldn't allow his partner to enter a place like Terror Castle alone, so he followed. They walked up the old marble steps and across a tiled terrace. As Jupiter was about to reach for the doorknob, Pete grabbed his arm.

"Wait!" he said. "Do you hear spooky music?"

Both boys listened. For a moment they had the impression they heard a few weird notes, sounding as if they came from a million miles away. Then in the darkness they could hear only the night noises of insects and of a small stone or two rolling down the steep sides of the canyon.

"Probably just imagination," Jupiter said, though he did not sound too certain of it. "Or possibly we heard a TV set playing over the ridge in the next canyon. Some trick of acoustics."

"Some trick, all right," Pete muttered. "What if it was the old ruined pipe organ being played by the Blue Phantom?"

"Then we certainly want to hear it," Jupe said. "Let us enter."

He grasped the knob and pulled. With a long *scre-e-e-ch* that curdled Pete's blood, it opened. Not waiting for their courage to evaporate, the two boys marched into a long dark hall, playing their flashlight beams straight ahead.

They passed open doorways, full of shadows, which seemed to breathe musty air at them. Then they came out into a large hallway with a ceiling two stories high. Jupiter stopped.

"We're here," he said. "This is the main hall. We'll stay one hour. Then we'll leave."

"Leave!" a voice low and eerie whispered in their ears.

Chapter 5

Echoes of Doom

"DID YOU HEAR THAT?" Pete exclaimed. "The phantom told us to leave. Come on, some things I don't have to be told twice."

"Wait!" His partner grabbed his wrist.

"Wait!" the ghostly voice said, more loudly.

"As I thought," Jupiter stated. "Merely an echo. This hallway is very high, you will notice, and it is circular. Circular walls make fine reflecting surfaces for sounds. The original owner, Mr. Terrill, built it this way on purpose. He called this Echo Hall, or the Echo Room."

"Doom!" the echo seemed to whisper in Pete's ear.

However, Jupe was right. You couldn't let an echo scare you.

"I'm just kidding," Pete said airily. "I knew it was an echo all along." And he laughed loudly to prove it.

Instantly weird laughter rang out around them. The very walls seemed to laugh *Ha-ha-ha-ha-ha-ha-ha! Ho-ho-ho-ho-ho!* The laughter died away into a final eerie chuckle, and Pete gulped.

"Did I do that?" he whispered.

"You did it," his companion whispered back. "But please don't do it again."

"Don't worry," Pete whispered. "Not in a million years."

"Come over here." Jupiter pulled him to one side. "Now we can talk," he said. "The echo only works when you stand in the exact middle of the hallway. I wanted to test it as a possible source of the fearsome manifestations mentioned by various observers in the past."

"You could have warned me," Pete said.

"Echo Hall was clearly mentioned in the research Bob did for us," Jupiter stated. "You just didn't read it carefully."

"I was reading that part about the family from the East who spent one evening here and then were never seen again," Pete told him.

"They may have just gone back east," Jupiter said. "However, it seems to be true that no one has spent an entire night in this building for at least twenty years. Our job is to learn what frightened those people. If it was a genuine phantom or spirit—a supernatural presence of the former owner, Stephen Terrill—we will make an important scientific discovery."

"What else could it be?" Pete asked.

He was flashing his light around the circular stone walls of the room. A staircase wound up to the floor above, but he had no intention whatever of going up that staircase. There were decaying tapestries on the wall, with carved wooden benches placed beneath them. In several shallow niches or alcoves stood suits of armor.

A number of large pictures hung on the wall. He let his light flick from one to another. They all seemed to be portraits of the same man in different costumes. In one he was an English nobleman. In others, he was a hunchback, a circus freak, a one-eyed pirate.

Pete decided they were all pictures of the original owner, Stephen Terrill, in some of his famous movie roles from the silent movie days.

"I have been testing my own sensations," Jupiter interrupted Pete's survey of the hall, "and at the moment I do not feel afraid. Merely a bit keyed up."

"Me too," Pete agreed. "Since those crazy echoes quit, it just seems like an old house."

"Usually," his partner said thoughtfully, "it takes a little time for Terror Castle to have an effect upon those who enter it. In the beginning they feel only a vague uneasiness. This is followed by a sense of great nervousness, which progresses to sheer terror."

Pete only half heard the remark. He was flashing his light over the pictures on the wall again when he saw something that gave him a sudden sensation of uneasiness followed immediately by a great nervousness.

The single eye of the one-eyed pirate in the picture was staring at him!

The bad eye was covered by a black patch. But the good one was definitely looking at him. It had a luminous, reddish shine to it, and as Pete stared he saw it blink.

"Jupe!" The word came from him like a croak. "That picture. It's looking at us!"

"What picture?"

"That one." Pete aimed the beam of his light at the pirate picture. "I saw it looking at us."

"Merely an illusion," his partner said. "When a painter paints a subject with his eyes looking straight ahead, they seem to be looking at you no matter where you are in the room."

"But it isn't a painted eye!" Pete protested. "It's a real eye. It's a painted picture with a real eye!"

"I'm afraid you're wrong," Jupiter said. "It's definitely a painted eye. But we'll go closer and see."

ing, followed. Now they were both shining their lights
He walked toward the picture, and Pete, after hesitat-
on the picture, and Pete could see that Jupiter was right—it was a painted eye. Very real looking but it didn't glisten the way a real eye would.

"I guess I was wrong," he admitted. "But I certainly thought I saw it blink. . . . Hey!" The word was just a gasp. "Do you feel what I feel?"

"I feel cold," the other lad said, sounding puzzled. "We've entered a zone of low temperature. Cold spots are very frequently found in haunted houses."

"Then this one is haunted," Pete Crenshaw told him, his teeth chattering. "I feel a cold draft as if a whole parade of ghosts were rushing by. I've got goose flesh. I'm scared! That's all. I'm just plain scared!"

He stood there for a moment longer, trying to control his chattering teeth. From nowhere the icy draft flowed over him. Then he saw faint, wispy tendrils of mist begin to form in the air as if a spirit might be materializing. At the same instant the uneasy feeling that had become extreme nervousness mounted to sheer terror.

He turned. He didn't intend to turn. His feet did it for him. They took him straight out the main entrance of Terror Castle and down the old driveway, running like a deer.

Right beside him was Jupiter Jones. It was the first time Pete had ever seen his partner run away from anything so fast.

"I thought you said your legs took orders from you," he called.

"They do," his partner called back. "I ordered them to run."

And run they both did, in great strides. Their flashlights made wild bobbing paths of light in front of them as they left behind the silent, brooding bulk of Terror Castle and that awful, uncontrollable feeling of creeping, crawling fear.

Chapter 6

A Ghostly Telephone Call

EVEN WITH HIS longer legs, Pete had difficulty keeping up with his racing partner. Then his heart gave an extra leap. He heard footsteps right behind them!

"Somebody——" he gasped. "Somebody . . . chasing . . . us."

Jupiter shook his head.

"Just . . . echoes . . . off . . . the wall," he panted.

To Pete the pursuing footsteps had an eerie quality that didn't sound like an echo—and didn't sound like footsteps made by anything human, either. But at that moment he and Jupiter left the wall behind, and the footsteps abruptly stopped chasing them. Apparently Jupe was right again. Just more echoes.

But it wasn't any echo that had caused the overwhelming feeling of terror which had gripped Pete back in the big round hall of Terror Castle. He knew that. He couldn't have kept from running for a thousand dollars.

They were slowing down now to get around the big

boulders that narrowed the road to a footpath. But still they kept on running. It just seemed like a good idea.

They rounded a bend in the road, and the dark, sinister building was no longer visible. Ahead of them, far down in the valley, the lights of Los Angeles twinkled. And there, parked a hundred yards down the road, was the car with Worthington, the English chauffeur, waiting at the wheel.

Pete and Jupiter had slowed down to a dogtrot when unexpectedly, from far behind them, came a shrill scream. It was a curious, piercing scream, with a gurgling, bubbling quality to it as if whoever was screaming had just—but Pete didn't care to think about what might have made the scream sound so funny.

They reached the big, waiting Rolls-Royce, its golden door handles and metal parts gleaming in the starlight. Somebody flung the door open, and Pete fell into the rear, where Bob was waiting for them. Bob pulled Pete up into the seat as Jupiter piled in behind him.

"Worthington!" Jupiter shouted. "Take us back home."

"Very good, Master Jones," the tall, dignified chauffeur said, and the big car purred into life. It began to sweep down the curves toward the valley below, faster and faster.

"What happened?" Bob asked as, puffing, the other two fell back onto the leather-cushioned seat. "What was that scream?"

"I don't know," Jupiter said.

"I don't want to know." Pete amended the statement. "And if anybody else knows, I hope he doesn't tell me."

"But what happened?" Bob asked. "Did you see the Blue Phantom?"

Jupiter shook his head.

"We didn't see anything. But just the same something scared us silly."

"Correction," Pete declared. "We were already silly. Something just scared us sillier."

"Then the castle really is haunted?" Bob asked eagerly. "All those stories are true?"

"As far as I'm concerned, it's headquarters for the Union of Ghosts, Ghouls, and Werewolves of America," Pete declared, breathing easier now as the car took them ever farther from the spot. "It's one place we're never going to go again, are we?"

He turned to Jupiter, who was sitting back, pinching his lower lip between thumb and forefinger, always a sign he was deep in thought.

"We *aren't* ever going back, are we?" Pete repeated hopefully. But Jupiter Jones did not seem to hear him. He looked out the window of the racing car and continued to pinch his lip without answering.

When the car finally reached The Jones Salvage Yard, Jupiter thanked Worthington and said he would phone next time he needed transportation.

"Better luck next time, Master Jones," the chauffeur said. "I must say I enjoy this kind of assignment. It's quite a change from driving for fat bankers and rich old ladies."

Then he drove off, and Jupiter led his partners into the junkyard. His Uncle Titus and Aunt Mathilda were inside their little house, which adjoined the yard. The boys could see them through the open window, watching television.

"It's still early," Jupiter said. "We returned from our expedition sooner than I had planned."

"But not half soon enough to suit me," Pete told him. He was still somewhat pale. Jupiter was pale, too. But the stocky boy could be very stubborn at times, and admitting that he was scared was one of the things he was most stubborn about.

Now he said, "I hope you recorded that scream on the tape recorder. If so, we can listen to it and attempt to identify it."

"You hope I recorded the scream!" Pete yelled. "I was running, not recording. Or maybe you didn't notice?"

"My instructions were to record all unusual sounds," Jupiter said. "However, under the circumstances, I suppose you can't be blamed."

Jupiter led them through "Easy Three," their code name for the easiest entrance to Headquarters. It was a big oak door, still in its frame, which seemed to be leaning against a pile of large granite blocks from a demolished building.

Jupiter walked over and fished a big, rusty iron key out of a box of junk, where no one would have given it a second look. He unlocked the oak door, pulled it open, and they ducked in.

Now they were in an old iron boiler that had come from some monster steam engine. They walked through it, slightly stooped, and at the other end crawled through a round door directly into Headquarters. Jupiter turned on the light and sat down behind the desk.

"Now," he said, "we must evaluate what happened. Pete, what made you run from Terror Castle tonight?"

"Nothing made me run," Pete told him. "I ran because I wanted to."

"I will phrase the question differently. What made you want to run?"

"Well," Pete said, "there in Echo Hall, I first began to feel uneasy. Just uneasy. After a little while, I was feeling extremely nervous. All of a sudden the extreme nervousness became sheer terror, and then I wanted to run."

"Mmm." Jupiter pinched his lower lip. "Your experience was exactly the same as mine. First uneasiness. Then extreme nervousness. Then sheer terror. And yet, what really happened? We heard some echoes—we felt a cold draft——"

"An ice-cold draft!" Pete corrected him. "And what about the picture that looked at me with a living eye?"

"Probably only imagination," Jupiter told him. "We actually saw and heard nothing to frighten us. Yet we felt frightened. The question is, why?"

"What do you mean, why?" Pete asked. "Any old deserted house is kind of frightening, and that place is so scary it would frighten spooks!"

"Perhaps that is the answer," Jupiter agreed. "We must visit Terror Castle again and——"

And then the telephone rang.

They stared at it. The telephone had never rung before. Jupiter had had it installed less than a week ago when they had definitely decided they would start some kind of business. They planned to pay the charges from the money they made repairing broken items for Mr. Jones. It was listed in Jupiter's name, but of course the listing hadn't been put in the telephone book yet. So far, no one else knew they had it. Yet here it was ringing!

It rang again. Pete gulped. "Well, answer it," he said.

"I will." Jupiter picked it up. "Hello?" he said into the phone. "Hello?"

He held the telephone close to a microphone and speaker he had put together from the parts of an old radio. This made it possible for them all to hear what was said. But all they could hear was a curious humming, far off.

"Hello!" he said once more. But there was still no answer, so finally he hung up.

"Probably a wrong number," he stated. "As I was saying——"

The phone rang again.

They stared at it. Jupiter reached for it as if someone was holding onto his arm for dear life.

"Huh-hello?" he said.

They heard the strange humming again, sounding far off and lonesome. Then they heard a voice that seemed to be gargling, as if the speaker hadn't talked in years but was trying hard to say something.

"*Stay*——" the voice said. Then, as if it were a great effort, as if it were the most tremendous effort imaginable, the voice got out another word.

"——*away*," it said. "*Stay . . . away.*"

Then it died out in a long gasp, and again there was just a weird humming noise.

"Stay away from what?" Jupiter asked the telephone.

But the telephone didn't answer. It just went on humming.

He hung up. For a long moment no one said anything. Then Pete stood up.

"I've got to get home," he said. "I just remembered something I have to tend to."

"Me, too." Bob hopped up. "I'll go with you."

"Possibly Aunt Mathilda would like me to do some

errands," Jupiter said, and he got up, too. They practically fell over one another in their eagerness to get out of Headquarters.

The voice on the phone hadn't finished the sentence. But they didn't have any trouble figuring what he—or it, or whatever it was—had been trying to tell them.

Stay away from Terror Castle!

Chapter 7

Trapped!

"WE HAVE A PROBLEM," Jupiter said the following afternoon. He and Pete were seated in their Headquarters office—Bob was busy at the library—and Jupe was scowling at a sheet of paper.

"In fact, we have two problems," The First Investigator added.

"I can tell you how to solve our problems," Pete said. "Just pick up that telephone and call Mr. Alfred Hitchcock and tell him we've decided not to find a haunted house for him. Tell him we break out into large lumps of goose flesh whenever we get near one. Tell him our legs go all wobbly and start running of their own accord."

Jupiter ignored the suggestion.

"Our first problem," he stated, "is to determine who made that phone call last night."

"Not who," Pete declared. "What. . . . Was it a phantom or a spook or a werewolf, or just a disembodied spirit?"

"Disembodied spirits," said his partner, "are not known to use telephones. Neither are spooks, phantoms, or werewolves."

"That was in the old days. Why shouldn't they change with the times and be modern, too? That voice last night didn't sound like a human voice to me."

Jupiter scowled, his round features showing puzzlement.

"I agree," he said. "The whole problem is made more perplexing by the fact that, except for us and Worthington, not a living soul knew of our visit to Terror Castle last night."

"But what about souls who aren't living?" Pete asked.

"If Terror Castle is actually haunted," Jupiter told him, "we wish to prove it. It will be a feather in our caps. We ought to learn more about Stephen Terrill. If he is the one who put a curse on the castle then presumably it is his ghost haunting the place now."

"Well, that sounds reasonable," Pete admitted.

"Our first line of action, then, is to locate someone who knew Stephen Terrill in the days when he was a silent-picture star, and who can tell us more about him."

"But that was a long time ago!" Pete protested. "Who'd we find?"

"It seems a long time to us because of our youthful years. There must still be many people in Hollywood who knew Mr. Terrill."

"Oh, sure. Name two."

"Our best bet," Jupiter said, "would be Mr. Terrill's business manager, The Whisperer."

"The Whisperer?" Pete exclaimed. "What kind of name is that?"

"That was his nickname. His real name was Jonathan Rex. Here is a picture of him."

The First Investigator passed over a photograph of a newspaper picture and story. Bob Andrews had copied it at the library on the duplicator machine. It showed a rather tall man, with a totally bald head and a long, ugly scar on his neck, shaking hands with a smaller, pleasant-looking, brown-haired man with a rather wistful smile. The tall man had slitted, ferocious-looking eyes.

"Wow!" Pete exclaimed. "So that was what Stephen Terrill looked like! He didn't have to do any acting to scare people. That scar and those eyes would freeze a guy in his tracks."

"You're looking at the wrong one. Mr. Terrill is the smaller man, the one who looks so friendly and harmless."

"Him?" Pete said. "He's the one who played all those ferocious monsters? That nice-looking guy?"

"He had a very average face, but he could twist it to represent any diabolical individual he desired," Jupiter explained. "The story says, in case you haven't read it——"

"I was concentrating on the ghostly parts," Pete confessed.

"Well, the story says that off the motion-picture set, Stephen Terrill was so shy, because of his lisp, that he could hardly talk to people. So he hired The Whisperer to handle all his business affairs. The Whisperer had no trouble getting people to agree to the terms he desired."

"I'll bet he didn't!" Pete declared. "He looks as if he'd draw a knife the minute anyone said no."

"If we can locate him, I'm sure he can tell us all we need to know."

"Oh, sure—*if*. Maybe you have an idea?"

"The telephone books. He may still be living in this region."

It was Pete who found the name.

"Here he is!" he exclaimed. "Jonathan Rex. Nine hundred fifteen Winding Valley Road. Shall we telephone him?"

"I think it would be better if our visit were unannounced. But we'll telephone for the car."

"That was a stroke of genius, winning that car," Pete said, as Jupiter telephoned. "I hate to think what we'll do when the thirty days are up."

"I have certain plans," his partner told him. "However, that's for the future. We'd better tell Aunt Mathilda we'll be late for supper."

Mrs. Jones agreed she would keep supper for them. But when Worthington and the big, gleaming car drove up to the gate of The Jones Salvage Yard, she shook her head.

"My sakes," she said, "I never know what you'll be doing next, Jupiter. Riding around in an automobile made for some Arabian sheik! You'll be spoiled, mark my words."

Just how her nephew would be spoiled, she didn't say. Jupiter did not seem worried by the prospect as he settled back onto the leather upholstery.

Worthington was forced to examine several maps before he announced he had found Winding Valley Road. It apparently started quite some distance away, on the other side of the range of mountains. As they started over the hills, Jupiter had one of his frequent inspirations.

"Worthington," he said, "I believe this road will pass within a mile of the entrance of Black Canyon."

"Yes, Master Jones," the chauffeur replied. "Just before we start over the hills to the valley."

"Then let's pay a quick visit to Black Canyon on the way. There's something I want to ascertain."

It took them only a few moments to reach the mouth of the narrow canyon they had visited the night before —and fled from so hastily. By daylight it looked better —but only a little better. As Worthington reached the spot where the rotted crossbars and rock slide had closed off the road, he gave an exclamation.

"Look!" he said. "Tire tracks over the ones we made last night! I hesitated to say it at the time, Master Jones, but I had an impression we were being followed. I could not be sure, however."

Followed? Pete and Jupiter stared at each other.

"Another mystery to ponder," Jupiter said. "But it must wait. Right now I want to look around the outside of Terror Castle."

"Fine!" The Second Investigator said. "Just as long as we stay on the outside it's okay with me."

By daylight they made rapid time, scrambling up the rock-choked, narrow road, until Terror Castle loomed above them.

"To think we went into that place after dark!" Pete said. "Wow!"

Jupiter led him all around the outside of the building, exploring even the rear of the castle and the steep slopes above it.

"We are looking for any evidence that human beings may be using this place as a hide-out," he said. "If they are, they are bound to leave some evidence—a trail in the dirt . . . a carelessly discarded cigarette. . . ."

But an extensive search found nothing. At last they stopped to rest up at one side of the building.

"Definitely no trace of any humans coming or going here," Jupiter said with satisfaction. "If the castle is inhabited, it can only be inhabited by ghosts. Which is what we want to prove."

"I'm satisfied to believe it without any proof," Pete told him.

At that moment, some very human shrieks made them whirl around so they could stare down at the front entrance of Terror Castle. While they watched, two figures came running through the door, yelling with terror, and raced madly down the road out of the canyon. One suddenly stumbled and went sprawling. Something shiny flew from his hand and fell beside the road. Ignoring it, he leaped up and raced after his companion.

"Well, those certainly weren't ghosts," Pete said, as his initial surprise diminished. "But they acted as if they had just met a couple."

"Quickly!" Jupiter was starting down the slope with surprising speed. "We must try to identify them."

Pete raced after him. Already the two runners were out of sight. Jupiter came to the spot where the one had fallen and picked up an expensive flashlight with a nameplate on it. Engraved on the nameplate were the letters E.S.N.

"E.S.N." Jupiter read. "Who does that make you think of?"

"E. Skinner Norris!" Pete exploded. "Skinny Norris! But it couldn't be! How could he be here?"

"Remember what Bob told us about Skinny hanging around him in the library, and about losing one of our professional cards? And what Worthington said about being followed last night? It would be just like Skinny to try to find out what we were up to, and then either beat us to whatever we were after or mess up the case for us."

"Yes," Pete agreed thoughtfully. "Skinny would do anything to get ahead of you for once. But if he and one of his pals went into Terror Castle, they certainly came out in a hurry!"

He chuckled, but Jupiter looked serious as he pocketed the flashlight.

"*We* came out in a hurry too," he reminded his partner. "The difference is, we're going back in, and I'm positive Skinny never will. In fact, I've decided to go back in right now and have a look around by daylight!"

Before Pete could protest, a crashing sound far above them made them look up.

A large boulder was plunging down the steep canyon wall toward them!

Pete started to duck, but Jupiter grabbed him.

"Wait!" he said. "It will miss us by some yards."

It did, hitting the road with an ominous crash ten yards away, splintering the concrete, and rolling on down the slope.

"If that had hit us," Pete said fervently, "Terror Castle would have had some new ghosts tonight!"

"Look!" Jupiter grabbed his arm. "There's somebody up on that slope, hiding behind bushes. I'll bet Skinny Norris climbed up there and rolled that stone down on us!"

"If he did," Pete said wrathfully, "we'll teach him better manners. Come on, Jupe, let's get him!"

Both boys began to scramble up the rough rocky slope of the canyon, hampered by loose stones and many scrub bushes. Above them a moving figure was disappearing in the distance. They rounded a sharp outcrop of rock and paused for breath. In front of them, going into the hillside, was a narrow, ragged crevice. At some time in the past, an earthquake had shaken these hills and split the rocks apart along a natural fault line.

As they stared at the opening, a sudden scraping sound above them drew their startled attention. Higher up on the slope, a mass of rocks and boulders was sliding down toward them.

Pete froze. But Jupiter acted without an instant's hesitation. He grabbed his partner's arm and yanked him forward, as deep into the narrow crevice as they could get. A moment later, with a thunderous roar, the sliding rocks and dirt passed over the mouth of the opening. A few rocks tumbled in. Enough others piled up on the flat spot in front of the crevice to make a solid wall, effectively entombing them inside the hill. The rest of the boulders roared on down to the road below.

Chapter 8

The Man with the Scar

AS THE ROAR of the landslide subsided, the boys found themselves in pitch darkness. The air was full of dry, gritty dust.

"Jupe," Pete said, coughing, "we can't get out. We're trapped! We'll suffocate."

"Breathe through your handkerchief until the dust settles," Jupiter advised him. He felt around until he found his partner in the darkness, and put a hand on his shoulder. "Don't worry about the air. This crevice must go a long way into the hillside, so there's plenty of air in here for now. Thanks to Skinny Norris, we at least have a flashlight."

"It's thanks to Skinny Norris we're here!" Pete exclaimed wrathfully. "Wait till I get my hands on him. I'll wring his skinny neck!"

"Unfortunately we can't prove it was he who rolled the rocks down upon us," Jupiter said.

As he finished speaking, a broad beam of light from the flashlight displaced the darkness. Jupiter slowly moved the beam around the entire crevice in which they found themselves. It was a kind of rough natural cave, about six feet high and four feet wide. To the rear it rapidly narrowed to a mere crack which, though it seemed to extend into the hillside for a long distance, could not be entered.

Where the mouth of the crevice had been, a huge rock was now jammed. Other boulders topped it and surrounded it, and the spaces between these were filled with dirt.

"Our exit," Jupiter remarked, "is effectively barricaded."

"Even at a time like this you use long words!" Pete complained. "Why don't you just say we can't get out? We're stuck."

"I won't say we can't get out because that fact remains to be proved," Jupiter said. "Help me push against these boulders. . . . If they can be moved——"

But they couldn't. Both boys thrust against the barricade with their full weight, to no avail. Panting, they paused to get their breath.

"Worthington will eventually come looking for us," Pete said gloomily. "But naturally he won't be able to find us. Then he'll call in the police and the Boy Scouts and they'll look for us. But nobody will be able to hear us yell through all this rock, and if they do find us, it'll be along about next week. And then—— What are you doing?" he broke off to ask.

Jupiter Jones was down on his knees, staring toward the rear of the crevice and using the flashlight beam to illuminate the area.

"I see ashes of a campfire under the dust," he said. "Obviously in the past some wayfarer used this crevice for a shelter."

He reached out, brushed loose dirt off something, and pulled free a stick about four feet long and two inches thick. One end had been whittled to a point. It was charred and burned, the point broken.

"And here," he said, "is the stick he used to hold his food over the fire. This is a very fortunate find."

Pete looked at the stick dubiously. It had been there a long time, and was old and fragile.

"That isn't strong enough to pry any rocks loose," he said, "if that's what you're thinking of."

"It isn't," Jupiter assured him.

When Jupiter had a scheme in mind, he usually preferred not to explain it in advance. He liked to see how his ideas worked before he talked about them. So Pete did not ask any questions as his stocky companion unhooked from his belt his prized Swiss knife, with its eight blades. He opened the large cutting blade and went to work on the charred tip of the stick.

When he had the point sharp again, he stood before the wall of rock and dirt which imprisoned them. Shining the flashlight beam carefully over the whole expanse, he picked a spot up near the corner of the rocky wall and inserted the point of the stick into the dirt. After a moment it met an obstruction. He withdrew it and inserted it a few inches away.

Then Jupiter gently twisted and pushed the stick, finding a crevice between some smaller rocks. After a minute or two the stick went forward easily. Jupiter pulled it back. Some dirt trickled back in with the stick. But both boys spied a tiny hole of bright daylight where it had been.

Jupiter returned to the job of probing the wall of rock and dirt. Time after time the stick met an obstruction, but he did not give up. After some minutes, he had pushed away enough dirt so they could clearly make out a small rock, about the shape of a football, near the very top of the wall.

"Now," Jupiter said with satisfaction, "if you will push on the lower left side of that rock, Pete, making certain to push toward the right instead of straight ahead, I believe we'll find my stratagem successful."

Pete stood on a loose rock, braced himself, and pushed as Jupiter had advised. At first the rock resisted. Then it gave way suddenly and popped out of place. It went on down the hillside and with it went a dozen other boulders, leaving a clear space almost two feet high at the top of the entrance to the crevice.

"Jupe, you're a genius!" Pete said.

"Please!" Jupiter winced slightly. "Don't call me a genius. I simply endeavor to exercise my native intelligence to its fullest ability."

"All right," Pete agreed. "But you got us out of here—or will have as soon as we crawl through that hole."

But when they were finally outside and brushing the dirt from themselves, a moment of doubt assailed the taller boy. "Golly, look at us!" he said. "We're a mess!"

"We can wash our hands and faces and get the worst dirt off our clothes at some service station," Jupiter decided. "Then we will continue on to Mr. Rex's residence."

"We're still going to see Mr. Rex?" Pete asked, as Jupiter led the way down to the road, now more rock-strewn than ever. They were heading back toward the spot where Worthington and the car waited.

"Yes," the First Investigator told him. "It is now too late to enter Terror Castle by daylight. We'll just have time to see Mr. Rex."

As they came into sight, Worthington turned toward them with an exclamation of relief. He had apparently been pacing back and forth beside the car.

"Master Jones!" he said. "I was beginning to worry. Did some mishap befall you?" he asked, eyeing the condition of their hands and faces and clothing.

"Nothing serious," Jupiter said. "Tell me, did two boys come out of Black Canyon about forty minutes ago?"

"Somewhat longer ago than that," Worthington said, as they climbed into the car. "Two lads came running this way, saw me, and ducked to one side. They entered some bushes down the road. Apparently they had concealed a car there, for a moment later a blue sports car roared off."

Pete and Jupiter looked at each other and nodded. Skinny Norris' car was a blue sports car.

"And then," Worthington continued, "I heard the sound of rocks sliding. When you did not appear, I began to fear for your safety. My orders are that I must never let this car out of my sight, but if you had not appeared in another moment, I would have come in search of you."

"You heard the sounds of rocks sliding *after* the two boys drove away?" Jupiter asked.

"Definitely after," Worthington said. "Where to now, sir?"

"Number 915 Winding Valley Road," Jupiter said, his tone absent-minded. Pete knew what was puzzling him. If Skinny Norris and his pal had driven away before the landslide, then who had pushed down the rocks that had imprisoned them in the crevice?

Pete glanced at his companion. Jupiter was pinching his lip, deep in thought.

"We seem to have solved the mystery of the other tire tracks," Jupiter remarked. "Obviously Skinny Norris made them. But then whom did we see in the canyon after Skinny and his friend ran away?"

"Maybe it was the little man who wasn't there," Pete said. "Anyway, it wasn't a spook, phantom, ghost, or spirit."

"No, whoever it was was human enough," Jupiter agreed. "When we come to a gas station, Worthington, we'd like to stop long enough to wash up."

After they had cleaned up, the car took them up a long, winding drive over the ridge of the mountains, then down into the broad valley beyond. They turned right, and after another mile found the beginning of Winding Valley Road. At first it was a wide, attractive drive, with expensive houses on both sides. But as it continued on back up into the ridge they had just crossed, it became more narrow and winding. In places the walls were almost vertical. At other spots there was barely room for a tiny bungalow or an old shack.

Still Winding Valley Road continued, rising higher and higher, getting narrower, until finally it came to an abrupt end against a steep, rocky slope, with a small turn-around area to enable a motorist to reverse his direction.

Worthington brought the car to a stop with an air of bewilderment.

"We've reached the end of the road," he said. "But I do not see any habitation."

"There's a mailbox!" Pete exclaimed. "It says *Rex-915*. The house must be around here somewhere."

He and Jupiter climbed out. The mailbox leaned beside a ragged bush. Behind it a rough trail of rocky steps led up the hillside, through other bushes and small trees. They started up this, and in a few moments they had left the car many feet below them.

Then they rounded a clump of shrubs and saw, tucked against the side of the hill, an old-fashioned Spanish bungalow with a red-tile roof. To one side of the bungalow, against the canyon wall, were several very large cages, and in these cages hundreds of parakeets were flapping and flying from perch to perch, keeping up a constant screeching sound.

As the boys stopped and stared at the cages of brilliantly colored birds, they heard footsteps behind them.

They turned and gazed with startled eyes at the man who was coming up the trail behind them. He was tall and completely bald, his eyes hidden behind huge black glasses. A livid scar ran across his throat from below one ear almost to his breastbone.

He spoke, and his voice was a sinister whisper.

"Stand right where you are! Don't move a step, do you hear?"

As they stood frozen, he came toward them, swinging in his left hand a great machete, its razor edge gleaming in the sunshine.

Chapter 9

Sinister Spirits

THE TALL, BALD MAN with the scarred throat approached them rapidly.

"Stand absolutely still, boys!" he whispered. "Don't move if you value your lives!"

To Pete, the warning seemed unnecessary. He couldn't move. Then the machete flashed through the air between him and Jupiter. It struck the ground somewhere near their feet, and the man gave an exclamation of disappointment.

"Missed!" he said.

The bald man took off his dark glasses, blinking at them with rather friendly blue eyes. He now looked a good deal less sinister.

"There was a snake in the grass behind you, boys," he said. "I don't know whether it was a rattler or not, but there are some around. I tried to get it with the machete, but I hurried too much."

He took out a red-and-white handkerchief and mopped his brow.

"I've been cutting the brush along the hill," he said. "This dry brush is a bad fire hazard. But it's hot work. How about joining me for a lemonade?" By now his hoarse, whispering speech seemed more natural to them. They judged it was a result of the same wound that had left the great scar on his throat.

Jonathan Rex led them into the bungalow. In a room which was screened on one side there were easy chairs and a table with a large jug of iced liquid in it. Beyond the screen were the cages of birds, which kept up their constant noise.

"I raise parakeets for a living," Mr. Rex explained as he poured out three glasses of lemonade and handed two to the boys. Then he excused himself for a moment and stepped into the next room.

Jupiter sipped his lemonade thoughtfully. "What do you think of Mr. Rex?" he asked.

"Why, he seems pretty nice," Pete answered. "I mean, after you get used to his voice."

"Yes, he's very friendly. I wonder why he said he was cutting brush with the machete, however? His hands and arms were quite clean. They would have had small twigs and bark on them if he had really been cutting dry brush."

"But why would he bother to make up a story for two kids he's never seen before?"

Jupiter shook his head. "I don't know. But if he had been out cutting brush for any length of time, how could he have a pitcher of lemonade with the ice hardly melted at all standing in here now?"

"Whiskers!" Pete exclaimed. "There's probably some easy answer. Maybe he likes lemonade."

"All answers are easy when you get them. It's only when you don't know them that they're hard."

Jupiter was silent as Jonathan Rex came back into the room. He had changed into a sport shirt with a collar, and he was wrapping a scarf around his throat.

"It bothers some people to see my scar," he whispered. "So I cover it when I have company. It's a relic of a little scrape I got into in the Malay Archipelago many years ago. But tell me, how do you happen to be calling on me?"

Jupiter produced a business card and Mr. Rex studied it.

"The Three Investigators, eh?" he said. "And what are you investigating?"

While Jupiter explained that they would like to ask him some questions about Stephen Terrill, Rex picked up his dark glasses from the table where he had placed them.

"My eyes are sensitive to daylight," he whispered. "I see best at night. . . . What is your interest in my old friend Stephen Terrill?"

"We wondered," Jupiter said, "if Mr. Terrill was the kind of man who would become a vindictive spirit, bent on haunting his former home to keep people out of it forever."

Behind the dark glasses the man's piercing gaze seemed to study them intently.

"A very good question," he said. "Let me answer it this way. My friend Stephen, though in his movie roles he played phantoms and monsters, pirates and weird creatures, was really very shy and gentle. That was why he needed me for his business manager. He couldn't bring himself to argue with people. Look at this picture."

He reached behind him for a large framed photograph that stood on a table. The two boys took it and studied it. It showed two men standing in a doorway, shaking hands. One of the men was The Whisperer. The other was not as tall, and was younger. Apparently it was the original of the picture they had seen in Bob's research notes.

The picture was signed: *To my good friend, J.R., from Steve.*

"You can see from that," Mr. Rex said, "why I handled all the business. I had a way with people—they didn't like to argue with me.

"That allowed Steve to devote himself to his acting. He took it very seriously. He enjoyed being able to thrill and scare audiences. When his poor speaking voice made his final picture such a laughing matter, it broke his heart. That was one thing he couldn't face—being laughed at. I'm sure you boys can understand that."

"Yes, sir," Jupiter said. "I know how he felt. I hate being laughed at, too."

"Exactly," the man whispered. "For weeks after the picture was released, Steve wouldn't leave his home. He sent the servants away. I did all the shopping. The reports kept coming in that audiences shrieked with laughter everywhere the picture was shown. I urged him to forget it, but he brooded about it.

"Finally he ordered me to obtain all the prints of his old pictures that were in existence. He was determined no one would ever see them again. I managed to get them, at considerable expense. I brought them to him. I had to tell him that the bank, which financed the building of his home, threatened to take the castle away from him. You see, he was a young man and expected to make many more pictures, so he had saved very little money.

"We were alone in the main room of the castle. He looked at me with burning eyes. 'They will never get me to go,' he said. 'No matter what happens to my body, my spirit will never leave this building.' "

The whispering voice ceased. The blank, dark glasses seemed like the eyes of some strange creature. Pete shook himself.

"Golly!" he said. "That certainly sounds as if he was planning to go into the haunt profession!"

"Yes," Jupiter agreed. "Yet, Mr. Rex, you say Mr. Terrill was a gentle individual. Such a person would hardly turn into a malevolent spirit capable of inspiring unreasoning terror in everyone who entered the castle."

"That's true, my boy," the man said. "But you see,

the unseen force that causes the sense of terror in everyone may not be the spirit of my old friend. It may be one of the other, much more sinister spirits that I strongly suspect now manifest themselves there."

"Other——" Pete swallowed hard "——more sinister spirits?"

"Yes, you see there are really two possibilities," Rex said. "You no doubt know that Stephen Terrill's car was found at the foot of a rocky cliff?"

The two boys nodded.

"And you have probably heard about the note he left in the castle, saying that it would forever be accursed?"

Both boys nodded again, their eyes fixed on Jonathan Rex's face.

"The police," Rex said, "were sure that my friend drove off that cliff on purpose, and I believe they were right. However, I never saw Steve again after that last conversation I just told you about. He sent me away after making me promise never to enter the door of the building again.

"What must his thoughts have been at the very end, when he wrote that note? Remember, in life his mission was to scare people. Now people were laughing at him. Might he not be determined that after death he would resume terrorizing them, if only to show he could not be safely laughed at?"

"You said there were two possibilities," Jupiter prompted him, when the strange, bald-headed man seemed to be about to fall into a deep meditation. "Also you spoke of other, more sinister spirits."

"Oh, yes," the man said. "When Steve built the castle, he sent all over the world for materials from various buildings supposed to be haunted. From Japan he obtained timbers of an ancient, ghost-ridden temple where a noble family had been wiped out in an earthquake.

"Then he bought material from a ruined mansion in England, where a beautiful girl had hanged herself rather than marry a man her father had picked out for her. And he imported stones from a castle on the Rhine, supposedly haunted by the ghost of a mad musician who was imprisoned in the cellars for many years. The musician was said to have displeased the ruling noble by playing music he did not like. After his death the tune which brought about his imprisonment was often heard coming from the locked music room of the castle."

"Gosh!" Pete exclaimed. "If all those dead characters are wandering around Terror Castle now, no wonder it's so hard to live in."

"They may be. They may not be," Jonathan Rex whispered. "I only know that even tramps, hoboes and thieves give Terror Castle a wide berth. Once a month I drive all the way over the hills to walk up the road, stand out in front, and examine the condition of my old friend's only monument. And in all these years I have never seen any sign of such persons around the building."

Jupiter nodded. That agreed with the observations he and Pete had made. He did not see any reason to mention the individual, whoever it might have been, who had rolled the rocks down on them.

"What about the newspaper stories that mention strange music from Mr. Terrill's pipe organ, and a Blue Phantom?" he asked.

"I can't say. I never saw the Blue Phantom. I do know that, even before his death, Steve mentioned that several times he had heard mysterious music coming from the organ in the projection room. As a test he locked the door and disconnected the electric apparatus which worked the organ. Still the music continued. But as soon as he entered the room, it ceased."

Pete swallowed hard. Mr. Rex removed his glasses and blinked at them.

"I cannot swear that Terror Castle is haunted by my old friend or anyone else," he whispered, "but personally I would not enter that front door and spend a night there now for ten thousand dollars."

Chapter 10

A Bad Slip

"JUPITER!" MATHILDA JONES'S VOICE rang out in the California sunshine. "Stack those iron rods against the fence. Peter! Help Jupiter carry the rods. And you, Bob, are you getting a tally of everything?"

It was a busy day at The Jones Salvage Yard. Sitting on an overturned bathtub, busy tallying everything, Bob Andrews wondered if they ever would be able to get into Headquarters for a meeting. It was two days since Jupiter and Pete had interviewed The Whisperer, and they hadn't been able to have a meeting yet. Mrs. Jones had just been running them ragged. And when she wasn't keeping them busy, he had his own work at the library and Pete had chores to do at home.

Mr. Jones had been off on a buying spree, so there was an endless supply of new material coming into the yard. At this rate a week might go by before they could have any peace in which to sit down and puzzle over some of the very mystifying questions with which they were confronted.

A break came about noon when Mrs. Jones looked up and saw the salvage yard's main truck turning in through the gates again. Jupiter's uncle, Titus Jones, a small man with a large nose and a huge black mustache, was sitting like a king on top of the load in a magnificent old carved wooden chair. When Mr. Jones was on a buying trip, he bought anything that took his fancy. Mrs. Jones gave a little shriek as the truck stopped. "Heavens above!" she cried. "Titus Andronicus Jones, what have you bought this time to take us one step closer to the poorhouse?"

Mr. Jones waved down to them with his pipe. His other hand was holding tight to a big fan-shaped bunch of metal tubes. It was a home-sized pipe organ, about eight feet tall.

"I've bought a pipe organ, Mathilda," Mr. Jones called out. He had a very deep voice. "I'm going to learn to play it. Come on, Hans . . . Konrad, we have to get this valuable musical relic safely deposited upon the ground."

Mr. Jones hopped down like a boy. Hans followed him, and Konrad slid the pipes of the pipe organ onto the iron loading elevator at the back of the truck. Once it was in place, Hans worked the control and the whole thing eased down to the ground.

"A pipe organ!" Mathilda Jones was so flabbergasted she forgot to order the boys to keep working. "Now in the name of goodness and mercy and sweetness and light, what are you going to do with a pipe organ?"

Mr. Jones took a puff on his pipe. "Learn to play it, my dear," he said. "After all, I played a calliope in a circus once."

With Mr. Jones bossing, Hans and Konrad got the rest of the parts of the pipe organ off the truck. The two brothers were Bavarians—each about six feet four inches tall and very blond. They could lift almost anything.

Mr. Jones decided to set the pipe organ up by the fence nearest to his house. Hans and Konrad hauled and heaved and carried, and eventually all the pieces of the pipe organ were grouped together, waiting to be assembled.

"That's a real pipe organ, the kind operated by air blown into the pipes," Mr. Jones proudly told the boys. "I found this choice item in a small theatre being torn down over toward Los Angeles."

"Heavens to Betsy above." Mrs. Jones sighed. "I'm certainly glad we're a long way from the nearest neighbors."

"Now you take a really big pipe organ," Mr. Jones said, "one built for a large auditorium. It is possible to install pipes in such a pipe organ so large, of such a length and diameter, if you follow me, that they will emit sounds too deep to be heard by the human ear."

"If you can't hear them, can you call them sounds, Uncle Titus?" Jupiter asked.

"Someone can hear them—perhaps elephants. They have very large ears," Mr. Jones said with a chuckle.

"What good would a pipe organ be, giving out sounds you couldn't hear?" Pete asked. "I mean, hardly any elephants go to listen to pipe organs play."

"I don't know, my boy, I don't know," Titus Jones said. "I imagine science could find some use for them if science really tried."

"After all," Bob put in, "for dogs they have whistles we can't hear. They blow such a high note."

"Exactly, my boy," Mr. Jones said. "Possibly a circus could make whistles for elephants which would be just the opposite of the dog whistles. Low notes instead of high notes."

"Subsonic," Jupiter put in. "Sounds, or rather vibrations too low to hear would be subsonic, or below sound. Sounds too high for a human to hear are ultrasonic."

They were all so interested in the pipe organ that no one noticed the blue sports car which came whizzing in the gate and skidded to a stop behind them. The driver —a tall, thin youth with a long nose—gave the horn a loud blare. All three boys jumped slightly as they turned. This was greeted by loud laughter from the driver and the two companions beside him.

"Skinny Norris!" Pete exclaimed, as he watched the tall youth slide out of the car.

"What does *he* want here?" Bob demanded.

The Norris family spent only part of each year in Rocky Beach, but as far as Pete and Bob and Jupiter were concerned, that part was still too much. Being very much impressed by his own intelligence and having the advantage of driving his own car, E. Skinner Norris tried hard to make himself the leader of those his own age. Most of the boys and girls in town ignored him. But he managed to collect a few cronies, who were attracted by his liberal spending and the parties he gave. These followers were enough to bolster his sense of self-importance.

Now, carrying a shoe box with a lid, he approached The Three Investigators while his friends watched, snickering. Just before he reached them, he whipped from his hip pocket a large magnifying glass and pretended to study the junkyard through it. Mr. Jones and his helpers had moved off with the pieces of the pipe organ by the time he spoke.

"Ah, yes," he said, in a very poor imitation of an English accent. "The right spot, I believe. Characterized by a low grade of junk found only in Jones's junkyard."

This humorous effort was greeted by laughter from the car. Pete clenched his fists.

"What do you want, Skinny?" he demanded.

E. Skinner Norris acted as if he had not heard. He turned the magnifying glass so as to seem to study Jupiter through it, then put it back in his pocket.

"Indeed, you can be none other than Jupiter Mac-Sherlock, the world-famous detective," he said, continuing his effort to sound English. "This is a fortunate moment for me. I have brought you a case that has baffled all of Scotland Yard. A despicable slaying of an innocent victim, which I am sure you will be able to solve."

Even as he handed the shoe box to Jupiter, all three boys felt sure they knew what was in it. Their sense of smell gave them advance information. Nevertheless, Jupiter opened the box and looked in at the contents, while Skinny Norris waited with a broad smile.

Inside the box was a large white rat from which life had long since departed.

"Do you think you can solve this horrid crime, Mac-Sherlock?" E. Skinner Norris asked. "I am offering a sizable reward for the capture of the culprit. Fifty trading stamps."

His companions in the car seemed to find this hilarious. Jupiter, however, did not change expression. He merely nodded in a slow and dignified manner.

"I can understand your desire to see justice done, Skinny," he said, "for I see that the victim was one of your best friends."

At this the laughter in the car stopped, and a flush began to spread over the thin boy's cheeks.

"My preliminary examination," Jupiter went on, "suggests that he probably died of indigestion brought on by trying to swallow the bragging of someone whose identity, at the moment, must remain concealed behind the initials E.S.N."

"You think you're smart, don't you?" Skinny Norris demanded angrily. It was his misfortune that his glibness usually deserted him just when he needed it most.

"Which reminds me that I have something for you," Jupiter said, putting the box on a pile of scrap. It was only a step or two to the office of the salvage yard. Jupe swiftly covered the distance and returned with the flashlight he and Pete had picked up in Black Canyon.

"This has the initials E.S.N. on it," he said. "Possibly they stand for E. Skinner Norris?"

"Or they could stand for Exceptionally Scared and Nervous," Pete suggested, grinning. "Been practicing your running lately, Skinny?"

"Give me that!" Skinny Norris snapped, and grabbed it from Jupiter. He turned and got back into his car.

"Investigators!" he jeered at the three boys. "What a laugh. Every kid in town will be in stitches at the idea."

The car wheels spun as he backed away and raced out the gate. Jupiter, Pete and Bob watched him go.

"I knew he picked up that card in the library," Bob said. "He knows all about us forming The Three Investigators."

"We want everybody to know," Jupiter said. "This just makes it more important that we do not fail on our first case."

He looked around. His uncle and Hans and Konrad were over by the wall, working on the pipe organ. His aunt had gone back to the house to prepare lunch.

"We are unobserved at the moment," he said. "If we hurry, we can hold a quick meeting before Aunt Mathilda announces lunch."

He led the way toward Tunnel Two.

And then it happened.

Absorbed in his plans, Jupiter stepped on a piece of pipe that rolled underneath his foot. He fell heavily to the ground. As he struggled to sit up, Bob and Pete could see him gritting his teeth.

"I've twisted my ankle," he said. And when he pulled up his trouser leg to investigate, they could see that his ankle was already swelling. "I'm afraid," Jupiter said reluctantly, "that I shall need medical attention."

Chapter 11

The Gypsy's Warning

WHAT A MESS!

It was two days since Jupiter had hurt himself. His
Uncle Titus had rushed him to the hospital, where they
had kept him a whole day, taking x-rays. Then they
had soaked his foot in some kind of bath and let him
come home. Doctor Alvarez said he would be able to
hobble around soon. In fact, he wanted him to exercise
his ankle as soon as he could.

But meanwhile there was Jupiter in bed with about
a mile and a half of bandage around his ankle.

And there was Mr. Hitchcock, maybe finding another
haunted house for his picture.

It looked as if The Three Investigators were going
to be out of business without ever being in business.

Pete and Bob, sitting beside Jupiter's bed, felt rather
low.

"Does it hurt?" Pete asked when Jupiter moved a
little and had to grit his teeth.

"No more than I deserve," Jupiter said, "for being

careless. Now let us proceed with our conference. The first subject to discuss is the mysterious telephone call we received immediately after our first visit to Terror Castle. Worthington has said he believes we were followed that night. Very likely Skinny Norris followed us."

"He could have, easy enough," Bob said. "He knew we were interested in the place."

"Skinny couldn't have telephoned us and made his voice sound like that," Pete objected. "So low and dead sounding. His voice is more like a pony whinnying."

"I agree," Jupiter said. "But it's the only possibility I have been able to hit upon."

He shifted his foot, wincing a little.

"Until I learn otherwise," he added, "I shall refuse to believe that disembodied phantoms can use telephones."

"Well, okay," Bob agreed. "What's next? The mysterious person who rolled the rocks down at you?"

"Yes," Pete said grimly. "What about him? He's one guy I'd like to get my hands on!"

"For the time being, I am ignoring him," Jupiter said. "We are now certain he was not Skinny Norris. He may have no connection with the case at all. It may have been a child or a man wandering in the canyon who started the rocks rolling by accident."

"He had an awfully good aim for someone who didn't mean it," Pete muttered.

"He must remain an enigma until further facts

emerge. I am thinking now of the untruths which Mr. Rex told us when Pete and I visited him. Why did he say he was cutting dry brush when it was obvious that he wasn't? And why did he have a pitcher of fresh lemonade ready, just as if he expected us to be calling on him at that very moment?"

Both questions stumped all three of them. Pete scratched his head.

"Whiskers!" he said. "The farther we go, the more mysteries there are."

At that moment Jupiter's Aunt Mathilda bustled into the room.

"I meant to tell you earlier," she said. "A queer thing happened yesterday morning just before you came back from the hospital. I forgot all about it in the excitement."

"Queer thing?" Jupiter asked, and they all pricked up their ears.

"An old gypsy woman came to the door. I don't know that I ought to tell you what she said."

An old gypsy woman! Now they really were sitting up.

"I'd very much like to know, Aunt Mathilda."

"Well, it was just nonsense anyway. But this tiny, little old gypsy woman knocked and in this awful, broken accent she said she'd read about your accident and had a warning for you."

A warning! From an old gypsy woman! The boys glanced at each other.

"Anyway," Mrs. Jones said, "I finally understood that she had been reading the cards, and three different times they gave her a message for you. It was the same message every time. You were to avoid the letters T.C., or anybody who had those initials. Your accident was caused by T.C., she said, and T.C. would bring you more harm if you didn't avoid them, or it, or whatever.

"I just laughed and told her she was right—T.C. stood for 'too careless'—and she went away. Poor thing, she looked so old and wild I don't believe she was right in the head."

With that, Mrs. Jones went back downstairs and left the three boys looking at each other.

"T. C.——" Bob's voice was hollow. "Terror Castle."

"It might have been someone Skinny Norris hired," Jupiter suggested, looking a bit pale. "Except that Skinny doesn't have that much imagination. Bringing me a dead rat is about his limit."

"Somebody——" Pete began "——correction, some-*thing* doesn't want us fooling around Terror Castle. First we get a weird warning over the telephone. Then this something uses a gypsy fortuneteller's cards to send us another warning. I think Mr. Something means it.

"Therefore, I propose we vote on whether or not to stay away from Terror Castle, as warned. All in favor, vote aye."

"Aye!" Bob said.

"Aye!" said Pete. "That makes a majority vote."

Jupiter looked at them. "Do you want Skinny Norris to have the last laugh on us?" he asked. "As of now, he's undoubtedly convinced we've failed as investigators. He's getting ready to tell the world so. Therefore, this is when we must act swiftly.

"Also," he added, "is it not apparent that these warnings add a new mystery to the case?"

"How do you mean?" Pete asked.

"No one else who investigated Terror Castle received any warnings. We are the first to be warned to stay away from it. This leads me to believe that we must be closer to the solution of the mystery of the strange terror that pervades it than we realize."

"Even if you're right," Pete argued, "what good does it do us? Here you are laid up. We can't do anything until you're on your feet again."

"That is not entirely accurate," Jupiter said. "Lying here last night, unable to sleep, I decided upon another course of action. The two of you must proceed to explore Terror Castle without me, while I lie here and ponder the different mysteries with which we are confronted."

"Me explore Terror Castle?" Bob yelled. "Just reading about it is as close to the place as I want to come."

"I don't expect you to find out too much, of course," Jupiter said. "But I hope you will experience the sensations of uneasiness that become extreme nervousness and then turn into sheer terror. Then, if you feel these sensations, I want you to test just how far you feel them."

"How far?" Pete yelped. "Last time I felt them from head to foot. From inside out and outside in. All over, in fact. What do you think—that my right hand is going to feel nervous while my left hand doesn't?"

"I mean how far from Terror Castle the feeling of terror persists," Jupiter explained. "After you depart from the castle, how far away are you when the terror leaves you? That is what I want to know."

"Last time it was about fifteen miles," Pete said. "When I got home and got into bed."

"This time, if you begin feeling a sensation of fear, distress, terror, or impending doom, I want you to leave slowly, in a dignified manner. Stop at intervals to see if the feeling is going away at all."

"Slowly." Pete laughed hollowly. "In a dignified manner."

"Perhaps you will feel nothing at all," Jupiter added, "as I wish you to go tomorrow by daylight. This time you will explore the building while there is still light. If you desire to, you can stand just inside the door when night comes, and see if the feeling of fear affects you there."

"Our pal," Pete said to Bob. "All we have to do is stand inside the door."

Bob heaved a sigh of relief.

"That lets me out," he said. "I have to work at the library tomorrow, and the next day, too."

"I'll be tied down, too, come to think of it," Pete said. "It's too bad, but I guess we just can't make it."

Jupiter Jones pinched his lower lip, putting the gears of his mental machinery into high. Then he nodded.

"In that case," he said, "we'll have to change the plan."

"Just what we've been trying to tell you," Pete said.

"There are several hours of daylight left," Jupiter said. "So you will have to have an early supper and visit Terror Castle today."

Chapter 12

The Blue Phantom

"DARN IT," PETE SAID, "when we have an argument, why does Jupe always win?"

"He won this one, all right," Bob agreed.

There in front of them was Terror Castle, perched on the canyon wall. Its towers, broken windows and covering of wild vines were sharp and clear in the late afternoon sunlight.

Bob shivered a little. "Maybe we should go in," he said. "It's only two hours to sunset. It'll be dark before we know it."

Pete looked back down the boulder-covered road. Behind the bend Worthington was waiting for them in the car. He had helped Bob over the worst rocks. Then he had had to return to guard the car, according to his employers' orders.

"Do you suppose Skinny Norris followed us this time?" Pete asked.

"No, I was watching behind us," Bob said. "Anyway,

Jupe is sure Skinny is going to give Terror Castle a wide berth from now on."

"But we have to prove we have more nerve than Skinny." Pete sighed.

Bob had the camera, and Pete was carrying the tape recorder. They both had flashlights attached to their belts. Together they climbed up the steps to the big front door. It was shut.

"That's funny." Pete scowled. "I'm positive Skinny didn't close the door when we saw him run out the other day."

"Maybe the wind blew it shut," Bob said.

Pete turned the knob. The door opened with a long *scre-e-e-ch* that made them jump a little.

"Just a rusty hinge," Bob said. "Nothing to make us nervous."

"Who said I was nervous?" Pete asked.

They went on into the hall, leaving the door open. Off one side of the hall there was a big room, filled with old furniture—massive carved chairs and tables and a huge fireplace. Jupe had told them to look around and take pictures. Bob didn't see anything very special about the room, but he took a couple of photos with the flash camera.

Then they went on to the round hall where Jupe and Pete had heard the echoes. It was an eerie, gloomy spot, with the suits of armor and the pictures of Mr. Terrill in fantastic costumes. But a few rays of sunshine coming in through a dusty window halfway up the stairs lightened the atmosphere a little.

"Pretend it's a museum," Bob told Pete. "You know how a museum feels. Nothing scary about that."

"That's right," Pete agreed. "This place does have that museum feeling—all dusty and old and dead."

"Dead-dead-dead-dead!"

The word rang in their ears.

"Wow!" Bob said. "The echoes!"

"Echoes-echoes-echoes-echoes!" the walls answered.

Pete pulled him to one side.

"Come over here," he said. "You only hear the echoes when you stand in that one spot."

Ordinarily Bob liked echoes. He liked to yell, "Hello!" and hear the echo answer back with a far-off *hello*. But somehow he didn't feel like testing the echoes in Echo Hall any more.

"Let's look at the pictures," he suggested. "Which one looked at you with a living eye?"

"Over there." Pete pointed across the room to a picture of a one-eyed pirate. "One minute the eye was alive, and the next it was just painted."

"That's something we can investigate," Bob said. "Stand on a chair and see if you can reach it."

Pete pushed a carved chair underneath the picture. But even on tiptoes, he couldn't reach the painting.

"There's a sort of balcony up above," Bob said. "The pictures are hung by long wires from the balcony. Maybe if we go up there, we can pull the picture up."

Pete started to get down from the chair, and Bob turned toward the staircase. Just as he turned, he felt somebody grab his camera by the leather strap hanging over his shoulder. At the same instant he caught a glimpse of a tall figure standing in the dark little alcove behind him. He let out a yell and started for the door —fast.

But he didn't get very far. The camera strap jerked him back, and he lost his balance, falling on his side on the marble floor. As he fell, he could see an enormous figure lunging for him. It was somebody in armor, swinging a huge sword straight down toward his head.

Bob gave another yell and scooted along the floor on his side. The great sword struck the floor with a clang, right on the spot where Bob had been lying. The fellow in armor followed, crashing onto the marble with a noise like a barrel full of tin cans falling over a cliff.

By this time the camera strap had finally worked its way off Bob's shoulder, so he kept on sliding along the floor until he came up against a wall. He looked back, expecting the man in armor to come after him. But what he saw instead practically made his hair stand on end.

The armored man's head had fallen off and rolled across the floor.

Then Bob took a closer look, and discovered that the suit of armor was empty. The helmet had come loose and bounced across the floor after him when the

suit of armor fell over. He stood up and dusted himself off. His camera was lying beside the armor, the strap still tangled in the metal links where it had got caught when he backed into the alcove.

He picked it up and took a picture of Pete, laughing his head off.

"Now I have a picture of the Laughing Phantom of Terror Castle," Bob said. "Jupe will enjoy this one."

"Sorry, Bob." Pete wiped his eyes and got back to normal. "But you did look funny pulling that rusty suit of armor after you."

Bob looked down at the armor on the floor. It had been standing on a little pedestal in the niche in the wall. Now it had come apart, of course. It was a little rusty but not in too bad a state. He took a picture of it. Then he took a picture of the one-eyed portrait on the wall, and a couple of the other paintings.

"If you're all through laughing," he said, "here's a door we didn't notice. It has a little sign on it that says ——" he had to squint to read the engraving on the little brass plate "——'Projection Room.' "

Pete came over. "Dad says that in the old days all the big stars had private projection rooms in their homes. They used them to show their own pictures to their friends. Let's see what it looks like."

Bob had to pull hard on the door. It came open slowly, as if somebody was holding it from the other side. As it opened, a little breeze of stale, damp air rolled out at them. The room beyond was as black as the inside of an alligator.

Pete unfastened his flashlight. It threw a strong beam, enabling them to see that the projection room was a big room, with about a hundred plush-lined seats in it. Far over the other side, they saw the indistinct outline of a large pipe organ.

"The place is all fixed up the way movie theaters used to be," Pete said. "Look at that pipe organ. It's about ten times the size of the one Mr. Jones bought. Let's look it over."

Bob tried his flashlight, but it wouldn't work. He had apparently broken it when he fell down. But Pete's flash gave plenty of light. They marched across the back of the projection room and up to the old pipe organ.

They weren't nervous now. Bob's comical tangle with the empty suit of armor had buoyed their spirits.

The old pipe organ, with huge pipes stretching up to the high ceiling, was dusty and covered with cobwebs. Bob took a picture of it for Jupiter.

They looked around some more. The plush seats were all decayed. Where the movie screen should have been, there were just some white strips hanging down. The longer the two boys stayed there, the staler and damper the air seemed to get.

"Nothing in here," Pete said. "Let's see what's upstairs."

They left the projection room, went back into Echo

Hall and started up the steps that curved around one side of the hall. Halfway up, where the sun was shining through the dusty window, they stopped to look out. The castle wall was right up against the steep, rocky sides of Black Canyon.

"We still have almost two hours of daylight," Bob said. "Plenty of time to look around."

"Let's have a better look at the pirate picture then," Pete suggested. "We can pull it up and see if there's anything funny about it."

When they reached the balcony they found that all the pictures were hanging from a molding just below the balcony. Together they grabbed the wires and began to hoist. The pirate picture had a heavy frame, but they finally managed to pull it up where they could turn the flashlight on it.

It was just an ordinary picture—a little shiny because it was painted with oil paint. Bob suggested that the shininess might have made Pete think he saw a living eye staring at him, but Pete looked doubtful.

"I thought it really was alive," he said. "But I guess I was wrong. Well, let's put it back."

They lowered the portrait into place and went up the next flight of stairs. They were going to start at the top and work their way down.

They kept on climbing flights of stairs until they found themselves inside a little round tower, high up on top of the castle. It had narrow windows, like a real castle, except that there were panes of glass in them.

The two boys looked down. They were above the top of Black Canyon, and for a distance of several miles they could see hills and more hills rising into the horizon. Then Pete let out an exclamation.

"Look!" he said. "A television antenna."

He was right. On top of the ridge nearest them was a television antenna, put up there by someone who lived down in the next canyon and couldn't get good reception.

"There's another canyon there real close," Pete said. "It isn't as lonely here as it looks."

"There are dozens of canyons running into these mountains," Bob told him. "But look how steep the ridge is. Nobody but a mountain goat could get over the top. You'd have to go around."

"You're right," Bob said. "Well, nothing up here. Let's start down and see what we can find that Jupe might want to know about."

On the floor below they came to a hall, and down the hall a door was open. They looked in. It must have been Stephen Terrill's library, the place where he left his farewell note, because there were hundreds of books on shelves. More pictures—similar to the ones down in Echo Hall, but smaller—hung on one of the walls.

"We better look this over," Pete decided, so they went in. The pictures were very interesting. They all showed Stephen Terrill in scenes from his movies. In every picture he looked different. He was a pirate, a highwayman, a werewolf, a zombie, a vampire, a monster from the ocean. Bob wished he could have seen the movies.

"They called him 'The Man with a Million Faces,' " he reminded Pete, as they went from one picture to the other. "Gleeps, look at that!"

They had come to a mummy case in a little alcove. It was a real Egyptian mummy case, like those often seen in museums. The lid was closed, and there was a silver plate attached to it. Pete turned his flashlight on the plate and Bob squinted to read what was engraved there. It said:

> THE CONTENTS OF THIS CASE
> WERE WILLED BY THEIR OWNER,
> MR. HUGH WILSON,
> TO THE MAN WHO GAVE HIM
> SO MUCH ENTERTAINMENT—
> MR. STEPHEN TERRILL

"Whiskers!" Pete said. "What do you suppose is inside?"

"Maybe a mummy," Bob suggested.

"Could be something valuable. Let's have a look."

They pushed up on the lid of the mummy case. It wasn't locked, but it was quite heavy. They had it about halfway up when Pete gave a yell and let go. The cover banged shut again.

"Did you see what I saw?" he asked.

Bob swallowed a couple of times. "I saw it," he said. "It's a skeleton."

"A nice, shiny white skeleton, grinning at us!"

"I guess that's what this Hugh Wilson willed to Stephen Terrill for giving him so much entertainment," Bob told him. "His skeleton. Let's open up the case so I can take a picture of it for Jupe."

Pete didn't much want to. But Bob reminded him that a skeleton was nothing but some bones and couldn't hurt anyone. They opened the mummy case again, and Bob was able to take a good picture of the grinning skeleton. He was positive Jupe would be interested.

While Bob was winding up the film and slipping in a new flash bulb, Pete wandered over by a window. He looked out and gave a yell.

"We better hurry," he said. "It's getting dark!"

Bob looked at his watch. "It can't be. It's more than an hour to sunset."

"Maybe the sun doesn't know that. Take a look."

Bob limped over to the window. Sure enough, it was getting dark outside. The sun was disappearing behind the canyon wall. The only reason it was still shining in the window was because Terror Castle was built so high up on the ridge.

"I forgot about the sun setting early in these canyons," he said. "That makes a difference."

"Let's go!" said Pete. "One place I don't want to be in is this place after dark."

They headed for the hall. As they looked up and down the long corridor, they saw that there were stairs at both ends. They couldn't figure out which set of stairs they had used before, so Pete finally picked the ones that were closest.

By the time they reached the floor below, the light was getting much dimmer. And they couldn't seem to locate a staircase that would take them on down. Finally they found a narrow set of steps at the far end of the hall behind a door.

"This isn't the way we came up," Bob said. "Maybe we ought to go back."

"All stairs go down," Pete answered. "And down is where we want to go—and fast! Come on."

They started down. As soon as they let go of the door, a spring closed it and they were in pitch darkness on the narrow stairs.

"We better find the way we came up," Bob said uneasily. "I don't like this darkness. I can't even see you."

"You don't like it. I don't like it. That makes it unanimous," Pete said. "Where are you?" His fingers reached for Bob. "Okay, let's not get separated. Back up and open the door."

Together they climbed back up to the door. But the knob refused to turn.

"I guess it locks on this side," Bob said, trying to sound calm. "It looks as if we have to go down this way whether we like it or not."

"We need some light!" Pete said. "If we could just find—— Hey, what's the matter with me? I have a flashlight—a nice new flashlight."

"Well, go ahead, turn it on," Bob urged him. "This darkness seems to be squeezing in on us. It's getting blacker, too."

"Correction." Pete sounded a little shaky. "I haven't got a flashlight, after all. Remember when we were shutting that mummy case? I must have left it there."

"Great," Bob said. "Wonderful. And mine busted when I was knocked down by that suit of armor."

"Maybe it was just shaken up," Pete suggested. "That happens."

His hands grabbed Bob's flashlight off his belt. Bob could hear him slapping it. For a long minute nothing happened. Then it came on. Not a real light, just a feeble glow.

"Bad connection," Pete said. "About as good as a candle. But it's light. Come on!"

They went down the narrow, winding stairs faster than Bob thought possible with the brace on his leg.

Pete led the way with the feebly glowing flashlight. At last they got down to where there were no more steps and decided they must be on the ground floor. Shining the light around as well as they could, they were just able to make out that they were in a small, square hall with two doors. As they were trying to decide which door to try, Pete grabbed Bob's arm.

"Listen!" he said. "Do you hear what I hear?"

Bob listened. He heard it.

Organ music! Faint, weird organ music. Somebody

was playing the ruined pipe organ in the projection room. Suddenly Bob felt the extreme nervousness that Jupiter had mentioned.

"It's coming from that direction," Pete whispered, pointing to one of the doors.

"So let's go that way." Bob pointed to the other door.

"No, this way," Pete said. "Because this way must lead us to the projection room. And we know the front entrance is outside the projection room. The other way might get us completely lost. Anything's better than that."

Pete pulled open the door and resolutely started down a dark hall, holding onto Bob's hand. As they progressed the music got louder, but it still sounded far away, like ghost music, full of screeches and wails.

Bob kept going because Pete wouldn't let him stop, but the closer they got to the music, the more extremely nervous he felt. Then Pete pushed open a door and they found themselves in the projection room itself.

They could tell it was the projection room because the dull glow of the flashlight gave enough light to show them the backs of the seats. Far down at the end, near the pipe organ, there was a blue glow. It hung in the air some four feet off the ground, more blob-shaped than anything else, and seemed to shimmer. As it shimmered, the ruined pipe organ gave out more ghostly wheezes and screeches.

"The Blue Phantom!" Bob gulped.

That was the moment when his feeling of extreme

nervousness that had become acute anxiety turned into sheer terror, just as Jupiter Jones had hoped would happen.

They raced across the room toward the door they knew was there. Pete shoved it open, and they were out in Echo Hall. Both boys headed for the main entrance, where the door was still open, and burst out onto the tiled terrace. Once there they kept going. But Bob's bad leg dragged a little and his foot hit a crack. He stumbled. Pete was running so fast he didn't notice. Bob went over, landing on a pile of leaves in a corner of the terrace, and instantly dug into them like a mouse hunting for cover.

As he waited for the Blue Phantom to come after him, his heart pounded like a compressed-air drill. And he was panting so loudly he couldn't hear anything else. When he realized that, he held his breath. And in the sudden stillness he could hear the Blue Phantom hunting for him. It was coming closer and closer, with little, slithery steps on the tiles. Its breathing was gaspy and ragged, strangely sinister and scary.

Suddenly the footsteps stopped. The thing was standing directly over him. For a long moment it stood there, still breathing in great gasps. Then it reached down and grabbed Bob's shoulder. When he felt it, Bob let out a yell that practically rattled the rocks down off the nearest hillside.

Chapter 13

The Sign of the Investigators

"AND WHAT HAPPENED after the Blue Phantom touched your shoulder, Bob?"

Jupiter was speaking. Inside Headquarters, The Three Investigators were holding their first meeting in three days. Pete had been away on a trip with his father and mother, to visit relatives in San Francisco. And Bob had been swamped with work at the library, recataloguing all the books. One other helper was out sick, so Bob had been working days and evenings too. Meanwhile Jupiter had been stuck in bed, letting his ankle heal, and reading books. This was the first chance they had had to get together in private.

"Well?" Jupiter asked again. "What happened?"

"You mean after I yelled?" Bob sounded reluctant to continue the conversation.

"Precisely. . . . After you yelled."

"Why don't you ask Pete?" Bob said, ducking the question. "It happened to him, too."

"Very well. *You* tell me what happened, Pete."

Pete looked sheepish, but obeyed.

"I fell down," he said. "Bob shouted so loudly when I grabbed his shoulder that I was startled and fell on top of him. Then he started to struggle and yell. He kept yelling, 'Let go of me, Phantom. You better go back inside where you belong if you know what's good for you.' My arms were all bruised trying to hold him until I could make him understand it was me, come back to see what had happened to him."

"Bob has the heart of a lion, despite his small stature," Jupiter said. "So you discovered he wasn't with you, and turned back to find him. He heard you breathing hard and thought it was the Phantom when you bent down to touch him. Correct?"

Bob nodded. He had felt rather foolish, there in the leaves, when Pete and he finally got untangled. For a minute he had really thought he was fighting the Blue Phantom.

Jupiter pinched his lip together. He was looking satisfied about something.

"And when you finally stopped fighting each other, you discovered something else," he said. "You discovered, did you not, that the feeling of extreme terror had disappeared?"

Pete and Bob looked at each other. How had Jupe figured that out? They were saving it up to surprise him.

"That's right," Pete said. "It had gone away."

"So the sensation does not extend beyond the walls

of Terror Castle," Jupiter said. "That is a very significant discovery."

"It is?" Bob asked.

"I'm positive of it," Jupiter said. "The photographs should be ready for examination now. Will you bring them from the darkroom, Pete, while I shut the ventilator? Uncle Titus is creating quite a racket outside."

He was right about his Uncle Titus. Mr. Jones had finally managed to assemble the pipe organ he had bought. While confined to bed, Jupiter had been reading a library book about pipe organs, and he had given his uncle a good deal of advice. Now Mr. Jones was testing the reassembled organ. He was playing "Asleep in the Deep," a favorite piece of Hans and Konrad's, and he was giving full power to all the deep bass notes, along with lots of quavery accompaniment to go with the main tune.

The boys had the roof ventilator of Headquarters open, so they were getting the full benefit of the playing. When Mr. Jones really dug down into the low notes, things inside Headquarters positively rattled. Bob felt as if the music was trying to lift him right out of his chair. It seemed to make him quiver all over.

By the time Jupiter had closed the ventilator, shutting out some of the din, Pete came back from the little darkroom with the prints of the photos Bob had snapped in Terror Castle. They were damp, but could be studied.

Jupiter examined them under a big reading glass. Then he passed them on to Bob and Pete. He spent the most time on the snapshots of Mr. Terrill's library and the suit of armor that had chased Bob.

"Very well done, Bob," Jupiter said. "With one exception. You failed to get a picture of the Blue Phantom seated at the keys of the ruined pipe organ."

"Did you expect me to walk down and photograph a shimmering blob playing an organ that can't be played?" Bob sounded a little sarcastic.

"*Nobody* would have stopped to take a photo," Pete said. "There was too much extreme terror in the atmosphere. Even you wouldn't have done it, Jupe."

"No, I suppose not," Jupiter agreed. "It is hard to act with composure when in the grip of fear. Still, such a picture would have done much to solve our problem."

Pete and Bob waited. Jupiter had had three days in bed to think, and he must have done a lot of thinking he wasn't telling them about yet.

"You see," Jupe added, "your adventure was very unusual in one respect. The Phantom of Terror Castle actually appeared to you before sundown."

"It was sundown inside," Pete told him. "It was darker than a black cat in a coal mine."

"Nevertheless, the sun was still shining outside. No one else has reported any manifestations before nighttime. Well, let's see what the other pictures tell us."

He picked up the one of the suit of armor.

"This armor," he said. "It looks fairly shiny, not rusty."

"It wasn't very rusty," Bob told him. "Only in spots."

"And these books and pictures in Mr. Terrill's library. They don't look very dusty."

"They were a little dusty," Pete said. "Not smothered in it, though."

"Mmm." Jupiter took a long look at the skeleton in the mummy case. "This skeleton. A most unusual legacy."

At that moment, the whole trailer that contained Headquarters seemed to shiver. A piece of iron stacked outside slipped and rattled against it. An extra loud blast from Mr. Jones's new pipe organ had almost lifted them off the ground.

"Wow!" Pete exclaimed. "I thought it was an earthquake!"

"Uncle Titus doesn't know his own strength when it comes to playing a pipe organ," Jupiter commented. "If he's going to keep on like that, we might as well break up this meeting. But before we do, here's something for you."

He handed each of them a long piece of chalk. It was like the chalk they used in school, except that Pete's piece was blue and Bob's was green.

"What's this for?" Pete asked.

"For marking trails with the signature of The Three Investigators." Jupiter took some white chalk and drew a big ? on the wall.

"That means," he said, "that one of The Three Investigators has been here. The white color tells that it was the First Investigator. A blue question mark would mean Pete, the Second Investigator, and a green one would mean you, Bob. If I had thought of this sooner, you wouldn't have got lost in Terror Castle. You could have marked your trail with question marks and followed them back."

"Gleeps, you're right," Pete said.

"Observe the simplicity of it," Jupiter told them. "The question mark is one of the commonest signs. If someone sees a question mark chalked on a wall or a doorway, he thinks some child has been playing, and forgets it. Yet to us, the question mark will convey an entire message. We can use it to mark a trail, indicate a hiding place, or identify the home of a suspect. From now on, never be without your special chalk."

They promised they wouldn't, and Jupiter got down to the meat of the meeting.

"I telephoned Mr. Alfred Hitchcock's office," he said. "Henrietta told me that tomorrow morning he is meeting with his staff to decide whether or not to go to England to film his picture in a haunted mansion over there. That means we have to make our report to him by tomorrow morning. Which means——"

"No!" Pete yelled. "I won't do it! As far as I'm concerned, Terror Castle is haunted and can stay that way. I don't need any more proof."

"While lying in bed thinking," Jupiter went on, "I have reached certain conclusions that must be tested. And we have to work swiftly to report to Mr. Hitchcock in time. Therefore, you must both get permission to stay out late tonight. For tonight we make our final assault upon the secret of Terror Castle!"

Chapter 14

A Ghost and a Mirror

TERROR CASTLE LOOMED in the darkness above Jupiter and Pete. There was no moon, just a few stars to relieve the ebony blackness of the canyon.

"It won't get any darker," Jupiter said, his voice hushed. "We might as well go on in."

Pete hefted the new, extra-powerful flashlight he had bought out of his allowance. His old one was still there, up in the library.

They walked up the broken steps and across the tiled terrace. Jupiter limped slightly, favoring his tightly taped ankle. Their footsteps seemed very loud in the darkness. Somewhere a small animal was frightened out of its hiding place and went streaking away from the beams of their flashlights.

"Whatever that is, it's a smart whatever-that-is," Pete said. "It's getting out of here."

Jupiter did not answer. He had his hand on the front door and was tugging. It wouldn't budge.

"Lend a hand," Jupiter said. "The door's stuck."

Pete grabbed the big brass handle, too. Suddenly something gave. The brass handle came off in their grasp. Together they tumbled backward and fell in a heap on the tiles.

"Oof!" Pete gasped. "You're lying on my stomach. I can't move. I can't breathe. Get off quick!"

Jupiter rolled over and got to his feet. Pete stood up, testing himself for broken bones or dislocations.

"I guess I'm still all here," he said. "Except my good sense. I left that at home."

His partner was examining the brass door handle under his flashlight.

"Look," he said. "The screw that holds the knob to the rod that goes through the lock came loose."

"Been a lot of traffic through here the last couple of weeks," Pete muttered. "Maybe it just wore out."

"Hmm." His stocky partner's face was set in a thoughtful scowl. "I wonder if it could have been loosened."

"Who'd do a thing like that?" Pete asked. "Anyway, we can't get in so we might as well go back."

"I feel sure we can effect an entrance elsewhere," Jupiter said. "Suppose we try one of those French windows down there."

He moved along the front wall of the building. Half a dozen tall French windows faced directly onto the terrace. The first five were securely locked. But the sixth was open half an inch. Jupiter pulled. It opened easily, like a door. Behind it was impenetrable darkness.

The darkness, however, was partially dispelled by Jupiter's flashlight. He pointed the beam in through the open window, showing a long table with chairs placed around it. At the far end of the table there were apparently dishes.

"The dining room," Jupiter said in a low voice. "We can enter here."

Inside, their flashlight beams roamed around the room, showing fine carved chairs, a long mahogany table, an elaborate sideboard and carved wooden paneling on the walls.

"There seem to be several doors," Jupiter remarked. "I wonder which we should take?"

"As far as I am concerned—— Ugh!" Pete let out a strangled exclamation as he half turned and saw a woman in long flowing robes looking at them. She wore clothes such as Pete had seen in pictures painted three hundred years before, and tied around her neck was a rope. The unattached end of the rope fell down across her robe to her feet. She had her hands tucked into her flowing sleeves, and was looking at the boys with an expression of sorrow.

Pete reached out and tugged at Jupe's jacket. "What is it?" Jupiter asked.

"L-look," Pete stuttered. "We aren't alone. We have company."

Jupiter turned and Pete felt him stiffen. That meant he saw her too—the woman who was watching them, not moving, not breathing, just standing there watching. Pete guessed he knew who she was all right. She was the ghost of the woman Mr. Rex had told them about, the one who had hanged herself to avoid marrying some man her father wanted her to.

For a moment the boys remained frozen. The ghostly apparition neither moved nor spoke.

"Shine your light that way," Jupiter whispered. "When I say 'now.' . . . *Now!*"

Together they turned their flashlights toward the standing woman.

She vanished, as silently as she had appeared.

There was nothing there now but a mirror, which reflected the light back into their eyes.

"A mirror!" Pete burst out. "Then she must have been behind us!"

He whirled around, zigzagging his light back and forth. But there was no one there. Except for them the room was empty.

"She's gone!" Pete said. "And I'm going too! That was a ghost!"

"Wait!" His stocky partner gripped his wrist. "Apparently we saw a ghostly reflection in a mirror, but we may have been mistaken. I'm sorry we acted so hastily. We should have taken more time to examine the unusual phenomenon."

"More time?" Pete yelled. "All right, why didn't you photograph her? You're carrying the camera."

"So I am." Jupiter sounded chagrined. "And I forgot all about using it."

"It wouldn't have shown anything anyway. You can't photograph a ghost."

"Likewise, a ghost can't reflect in a mirror," Jupe told him. "But either this one did, or else she was inside the mirror itself. I never heard of a mirror ghost. I wish she'd show herself again."

"That's your opinion, not mine," Pete retorted. "All right, we've proved Terror Castle is haunted. Now let's go tell Mr. Hitchcock."

"We have just begun," Jupiter said. "There is much to be learned yet. We must proceed farther. This time I won't forget the camera. I am very anxious to photograph the Blue Phantom playing the ruined pipe organ."

His partner's calmness helped to steady Pete. He shrugged.

"All right," he said. "But aren't you going to mark our route with the chalk?"

Jupiter gave another exclamation of annoyance.

"You're quite right," he said. "I shall repair the omission at once."

He stepped to the window by which they had entered and chalked a large question mark on it. Then he chalked a similar mark lightly on the dining room table, being careful not to mar the surface. After that he stepped to the big mirror on the wall to put The Three Investigators' special mark on it.

"So that if Worthington and Bob should come after us, they will have their attention drawn to it," he told

Pete as he pressed hard to make the chalk show on the polished glass.

"In case we're never seen again, you mean?" Pete asked.

Jupiter did not answer.

Under the pressure of his hand, the tall mirror had swung silently back, like a door. Beyond it lay a dark passageway, leading deep into Terror Castle.

Chapter 15

The Fog of Fear

THE TWO BOYS stared at the dark passage in astonishment.

"Golly!" Pete said. "A secret passage!"

"Hidden behind a mirror." Jupiter's brow was furrowed. "We must investigate it."

Before Pete could utter a protest, the stocky First Investigator had stepped through the opening where the mirror had swung back. And he was playing a beam of light down the long, narrow passage. It seemed to be just a hallway. The walls were rough stone, and there were no doorways, except at the far end.

"Come on," Jupiter said. "We must discover where this passage leads."

Pete joined him. He didn't exactly want to enter that secret passage and he didn't want to be left alone, either. It was better to have company, he decided.

Jupiter was carefully examining the stone walls with his flashlight. Now he turned back and began to examine the mirror-door. It appeared to be a normal mirror, set into the surface of a concealed wooden door. There was no knob, and no latch.

"Curious," he muttered. "There must be some secret means of opening the door."

He swung it shut. There was a firm click. And they were shut into the narrow passageway.

"Now you've done it!" Pete yelled. "You've locked us in!"

"Hmm." His partner tried to find some finger hold by which to pull the door open. There was none. The back was smooth wood, fitting snugly so that there was scarcely a crack into which to insert a fingernail.

"Definitely, there must be a secret means of opening the door," he said. "I wonder why it opened so easily when I touched it just a minute ago?"

"Never mind that," Pete told him. "Let's see you open it easily *again*. I want to get out."

"I'm sure that if an emergency arose, we could break through this wood, and then through the glass mirror," Jupiter said, running his fingertips over the wooden backing of the door. "However, it should not be necessary. We want to go in the other direction."

Pete was on the point of telling him that the opinions expressed were not necessarily those of the Second Investigator, but already Jupe was moving down the narrow passageway, tapping the walls with his knuckles.

"Solid," he remarked as he moved along. "But there is a suggestion of hollowness beyond the stone. Listen."

He rapped again. Pete listened. And he heard something.

He heard the far-off sound of the big ruined pipe organ beginning to play. The weird, wheezing tones seemed to fill the narrow passage, coming from all directions at once.

"Listen to that!" Pete exclaimed. "The Blue Phantom plays again!"

"I hear it," the other boy told him. Jupiter put his ear against the wall of the passage and held it there for a long moment.

"The music seems to be coming through the stone wall," he stated. "I'd say we are probably directly behind the ruined pipe organ in the projection room."

"You mean the Blue Phantom is on the other side of that wall?" Pete yelped.

"I hope so," Jupiter said. "After all, the whole purpose of tonight's expedition is to meet the Phantom and take his picture. And if possible interview him."

"Interview him?" Pete groaned. "You mean actually talk to him?"

"If we can catch him."

"But suppose he catches us?" Pete demanded. "That's what worries me."

"I must repeat"—Jupiter sounded rather severe now —"that according to all available records, the Blue Phantom has never harmed anyone. I am basing my entire strategy upon this point. During my stay in bed, I came to some conclusions about this case. I have kept them to myself, in order to verify them. I think we will soon find out whether I am correct or not."

"But suppose you're wrong?" Pete asked. "If you're wrong and the Blue Phantom decides he wants us to join his gang of spooks, then what?"

"Then I will admit I was wrong," Jupiter said. "But I will make one prediction now. In a few moments we will begin to feel a sensation of extreme terror."

"In a few moments!" Pete yelled. "What do you think I'm feeling now?"

"Merely great nervousness. The extreme terror is about to come."

"In that case I'm about to go. Come on, let's bust that mirror and get out of here."

"Wait!" Jupiter gripped his wrist. "Let me remind you that fear and terror are merely feelings. You will be terrified, but I assure you, no harm will come of it."

While Pete was trying to answer that, he became aware of a strange change inside the secret passage. Unnoticed, while they listened to the weird music beyond the wall, curious wisps of fog had suddenly appeared in the air. They were all over—along the floor, along the walls, along the ceiling.

Pete flashed his light up and down. In the bright beam the wisps of fog swirled slowly, coming together in weirdly sinuous coils and circles. As he stared at them, they seemed to form strange and sinister forms in the air.

"Look!" Pete's voice wavered. "I can see faces! And

there's a dragon—and a tiger—and a fat pirate . . ."

"Steady!" Jupiter said. "I can see strange images too, but they are just the product of our imagination. It's the same as lying on a hillside and watching the clouds. The eye turns them into all kinds of creatures. This mist is perfectly harmless. But I believe the extreme terror is about to begin."

He gripped Pete's hand hard, and Pete gripped back. Jupiter was right. Suddenly he felt fingers of terror running into every part of his body, from his scalp down to his toes. His skin seemed to quiver with the awful sensation. Only the fact that Jupiter must be feeling it too, and was standing as steady as a rock, kept Pete from racing back and hammering wildly on the mirror that blocked the passage.

As the sensation of terror swept over them, the fog thickened, twisting and turning in fantastic images in the air.

"The Fog of Fear," Jupiter said. His voice shook a little, but he stepped forward firmly. "Reported once before, many years ago. The ultimate manifestation of Terror Castle. Now let us try to get out and catch the Blue Phantom while he thinks we are paralyzed with fear."

"I can't," Pete managed to mumble through his clenched teeth. "I *am* paralyzed. I can't make my legs move."

Jupiter paused. "The time has come to tell you what I deduced while forced to stay in bed, Pete," he said.

"I deduced that Terror Castle is really haunted——"

"That's what I've been telling you all along!"

"——is really haunted, but not by a ghost. It's haunted by a man who is very much alive. In fact, the Phantom of Terror Castle, according to my deductions, is Mr. Stephen Terrill, the supposedly dead movie star himself."

"What?" Pete was so surprised he forgot the feeling of terror. "You mean alive and living here all these years?"

"Exactly. A living ghost. Scaring people away from his home so that he will not lose it."

"But how could he?" Pete asked. "I mean, we both know there's no sign that anybody ever comes or goes from here. How'd he get food and supplies?"

"I don't know. That's one thing I want to ask him. But now you understand—he has been scaring us on purpose just to keep us away. He doesn't really want to hurt anybody. Does that make you feel better?"

"Well, sure," Pete said. "Even though I still have that feeling of my legs wanting to go some place else."

"Then let us complete our investigation by unmasking the phantom," Jupiter said.

He started for the door at the end of the passage and Pete found himself keeping step. Now that Jupe had explained it, the whole thing made sense. Stephen Terrill himself, the master of terror, living in the old castle all these years, frightening people away!

They reached the door at the end of the passage. To

their surprise, it opened easily. They stepped through into pitch darkness. The weird music was louder now, and from its echoes they knew they must be in a much bigger room.

"The projection room," Jupiter whispered. "Don't use your light. We want to surprise the Phantom."

Side by side they felt their way along a wall and around a corner. Pete almost let out a wild yell when something soft and slithery swooped down and wrapped itself around his face and head. But it was just a rotten velvet drape that he had torn loose. He managed to free himself without making any noise.

Then they rounded a corner and there, halfway up the big room they saw a shimmering blob of misty blue light where the ruined pipe organ stood. They paused. In the darkness, Pete could feel his companion getting his flash camera set.

"We're going to sneak up on him," Jupiter whispered, "and take his picture."

Pete looked at the shimmering light, and suddenly felt sorry for Mr. Terrill. After all these years alone in this spooky castle, it was going to be a very great shock to him to be unmasked.

"We might scare him," he whispered back. "Why don't we call out his name, so he'll know we're here, and give him a chance to understand that we only want to be friendly?"

"A very sound idea. . . . We'll walk slowly toward him, while I call out to him."

They began to move toward the blob of light and the spooky music.

"Mr. Terrill!" Jupiter shouted. "Mr. Terrill, we want to talk to you. We're friends."

Nothing happened. The music kept on wheezing and wailing, and the blue blob kept on shimmering. They crept up another few feet and Jupiter tried again.

"Mr. Terrill," he called. "I'm Jupiter Jones. Pete Crenshaw is with me. We just want to talk to you."

At that, the music suddenly stopped.

The shimmering blue blob moved. It soared gracefully upward, toward the ceiling, and hung there.

As Jupiter and Pete stood gaping up at the unexpected flight of the ghostly organist, they were suddenly aware that someone was beside them in the darkness. Jupiter was taken totally by surprise, his camera still in his hand. Pete had just time enough to jam the "on" button of his flashlight into position. The beam of light revealed two men, one of average height, one quite short, both dressed in the flowing burnooses of Arabs. Each of the men was casting something white into the air.

A large net came down over Pete's head. It knocked the flashlight from his hand, putting it out, and enveloped him all the way to his feet.

He tried to run, caught his foot in the meshes of the net, and fell to the carpeted floor. He rolled over, struggling desperately, and realized he was as thoroughly trapped as any fish in a landing net. The more he struggled, the more tightly he bound himself in the clinging loops of the net.

"Jupe!" he yelled. "Help!"

His partner did not answer. Rolling over and twisting his neck, Pete could see why.

The two men had picked Jupiter up between them like a sack of potatoes. He, too, was thoroughly wrapped in a clinging net. Using a small lantern for light, they carried the stocky boy by his shoulders and legs across the room and disappeared through a door. His weight seemed to give them a certain amount of trouble.

Hardly able to move inside the net that had trapped him, Pete lay on the floor and could see nothing in the darkness except the blob of light that shimmered high above him, up against the ceiling.

It seemed to be pulsing—first getting larger, then smaller—exactly as if the Blue Phantom was laughing at him.

Chapter 16

Prisoners in the Dungeon

PRESENTLY THE BLUE PHANTOM faded out and was gone. Darkness like a blanket pressed down on Pete. He tried once more to wriggle free and only got himself more tightly tangled in the big net.

What a fix! he thought glumly. Instead of nabbing a harmless old fellow who was playing at being a ghost, they had been nabbed themselves. The two characters who had netted them had looked plenty tough. And they had obviously been ready and waiting.

Pete thought of Bob and Worthington waiting for them down the canyon road. Would he ever see them again? Would he ever see his Mom and Dad?

He was feeling as miserable as he had ever felt in his life when a light began bobbing across the room toward him. As it came closer, he saw that it was an electric lantern in the hand of a tall man. This one was wearing the long silk robes of an Oriental nobleman.

The man reached Pete and bent over him, shining

the lantern in his face. Pete could see cruel slant eyes and a mouth full of gold teeth.

"Small fools," the man said. "Why could you not be sensible and stay away, like the others? Now we must take care of you."

He drew a finger across his throat and made an ugly noise. Pete got the message. His blood ran cold.

"Who are you?" he asked. He stuttered a little, getting the words out. "What are you up to?"

"Ha!" the man said. "To the lower dungeon!" He picked Pete up like a sack of potatoes, threw him over his shoulder and started back the way he had come.

Slung over the man's shoulder, Pete couldn't see much in the almost total darkness. He knew they went through a door, down a passage, then down a very long flight of winding stairs. They came out in a corridor that felt damp and chilly, went through some more doors, and wound up in a small room like a cell. A dungeon cell. There were rusty ring-bolts attached to the walls.

Something white, like a cocoon, was lying in a corner. The smaller Arab sat beside it, sharpening a long knife.

"Where is Abdul?" the Oriental asked. He dumped Pete on the stone floor beside the cocoon, which turned out to be Jupiter, still wrapped in the net which had caught him.

"He went to get Zelda," the small Arab said in a deep, guttural voice. "She and Gypsy Kate are hiding

the pearls. We are going to take a vote on what we shall do with these puppies we have caught."

"I say we just lock the door to this cozy little room and leave them," the second man said. "No one will ever find them, and soon the old castle will really be haunted."

"It's not a bad idea." The Arab grunted. "But just to make certain, we ought to let a little blood first."

He ran the edge of his knife along his thumb, and Pete, watching him, swallowed with difficulty. He wanted to whisper to his stocky partner, but Jupiter was lying so still beside him that Pete was afraid he might be hurt.

"I'll go see where Zelda is." The Arab sheathed his knife and stood up. He cast a glance at the two bundles on the floor. "Come along and give me a hand hiding our tracks. These fish won't get out of the nets very fast."

"You're right. We must make haste." The tall Oriental hung his electric lantern on the wall so that it clearly illuminated the two boys. Then the two men hurried out. Pete could hear their footsteps growing fainter. Then he heard a grinding sound, as of a large rock being rolled. Then silence—until Jupiter spoke.

"Pete," he asked, "are you all right?"

"It depends on what you mean by all right," Pete told him. "If you mean no broken bones, yes, I'm fine, I'm dandy, I'm peachy-pie."

"I'm glad you have not been injured." Jupiter sounded

very upset. "I must apologize for leading you into unsuspected danger. I was too sure of my own deductions."

"Aw, it could happen to anybody," Pete answered. "I mean, it sounded so logical. Who could guess we were going to run into some kind of gang? Especially when we didn't find any traces outside of anybody using this place as a hangout."

"Yes, and I was so sure Mr. Terrill must be the one who was responsible," Jupiter said, "that it never occurred to me to suspect otherwise. Tell me, can you move your hands?"

"I can wiggle my little finger, if that's any help," Pete said. "I'm all tangled up in these meshes."

"Fortunately I have the use of my right hand," Jupiter told him. "I am making some progress toward freeing myself. Maybe you can help by telling me where to cut next."

Pete flopped over on his side. Jupe did likewise. Now that his partner's back was toward him, Pete could see that Jupiter had managed to get at the Swiss knife that hung from his belt. Its eight blades included a screwdriver and a pair of scissors. Jupiter had opened the tiny pair of scissors and had snipped several of the net's meshes so that he could get his hand out.

"Cut over toward your left," Pete whispered. "You'll be able to get your left hand free. . . . That's it."

The scissors were small and the net seemed to be made of tough nylon, but with Pete directing Jupiter made progress. Soon he had both hands free. After that he was able to make much faster progress. He was starting to cut off the whole bottom half of the net when they suddenly heard footsteps.

For a moment they were too terrified to move. Then Jupiter's wits began to work, and he rolled quickly over onto his back to hide the cut net. They waited with pounding hearts.

In a moment a stooped old crone came into the room, holding an electric lantern high over her head. She wore tattered gypsy robes and had huge gold rings in her ears.

"Well, my pretties," she cackled, "resting nice and comfortably? So you wouldn't take the warning that Gypsy Kate, good Gypsy Kate, went to so much trouble to leave you! And now look what's happened to you. Always heed a gypsy's warning, my pretties, and you'll be the better for it."

Something about the stiffness with which they lay attracted her attention, for she hurried directly to their sides.

"Tricks, my pretties, tricks?" she cackled. Deftly she turned Jupiter over and saw the cut net.

"So that's it! The chicks want to escape!" She grasped Jupiter's wrist and twisted it. The knife fell to the floor. She scooped it up. "Now we must teach you a lesson, pretty ones," she said, and raised her voice. "Zelda!" she screamed. "Ropes! Ropes! Our birdies want to fly away."

"I'm coming, Kate, I'm coming," a voice answered in English accents. In a moment a tall woman—well dressed—appeared in the doorway. She held a length of rope in her hand.

"They're clever, very clever," the old gypsy crooned. "We must tie them tightly, tightly. You help hold this one while I truss him up."

Pete could do nothing but watch as the two women made short work of securing his partner again. First they cut the net loose from Jupiter, then tied his hands securely behind his back. Next they tied his feet. Finally they ran a rope from his wrists to a rusty old iron ring set into the stone wall.

Since the net that held Pete was still intact, they just wound the rope around him a few times and tied it well.

"Now they'll stay, Zelda," the old gypsy cackled. "They'll never leave. I've convinced the men we mustn't be cruel. Oh no, we mustn't be cruel, we mustn't spill blood. We'll just leave them and close the door to this dungeon cell. They'll never tell anyone what has happened."

"It's a pity," the Englishwoman said. "They seem like nice boys."

"Don't get soft now, Zelda," the gypsy screeched. "We voted, and you can't go against the vote. Hurry now, we must hide our tracks and be gone."

She took the light from the wall and scurried out. The Englishwoman held the other lantern and played its beam down on the two helpless boys.

"Why did you have to be so stubborn, ducks?" she asked. "Everyone else got scared and stayed away. One little tune from the terror organ, and no one else has ever returned. Why did you have to be stubborn and keep coming back?"

"The Three Investigators never give up," Jupiter said stubbornly.

"Sometimes it's more sensible to give up," the woman replied. "Well, it's time for me to say good-bye. I hope you won't be frightened in the dark. I have to go now."

"Before you go," Jupiter said—and Pete had to admire the way he kept his voice steady—"may I ask a question?"

"To be sure, boy, to be sure," the woman said.

"What criminal enterprise are you and your confederates engaged in?" Jupiter asked.

"La, such long words!" The woman laughed. "Why, young man, we are smugglers. We smuggle valuables from the Orient, mostly pearls, and use this old place as our headquarters. For years we've kept everyone from coming near it by making it seem haunted. It's the perfect hiding place."

"But why do you wear such noticeable costumes?" the boy asked. "Anyone who sees you is bound to notice you."

"No one sees us, young man," the Englishwoman said. "And I mustn't answer all your questions or you won't have anything to think about. Good-bye now, in case we never meet again. And I don't think we will."

She took the electric lantern and hurried out. As she slammed the cell door shut, darkness wrapped itself around the two. Pete felt his throat getting dry and his tongue sticking to the roof of his mouth.

"Jupe," he said, "say something! I want to hear some noise."

"Oh, I'm sorry." Jupiter sounded absent-minded. "I was thinking."

"Thinking! At a time like this?"

"Why, yes. Did you notice that when Gypsy Kate left us a few minutes ago she turned to the right and went down the corridor in that direction?"

"No, I didn't notice. What difference does it make?"

"Well, that's the opposite direction from which we came. So she's not going back upstairs into the castle. She's going deeper into the dungeon. That suggests there must be a secret entrance somewhere. Which would also explain why there's no sign of anyone going in and out outside."

Whiskers! Even tied up in a dungeon and left to starve, Jupiter couldn't keep his gray cells from buzzing.

"I don't suppose while you've been doing all that thinking," Pete said, "you've thought of any way to get us out of here?"

"No," Jupiter said. "I haven't. I can't think of a single, solitary way for us to get out of here unassisted. Please accept my apologies, Pete. I made a bad miscalculation in this case."

Pete couldn't think of anything to say to that, and in silence the two boys lay and listened to the tiny sounds in the darkness. Somewhere a mouse scampered. And somewhere else water was dripping. The slow drops, as they fell, seemed to be measuring off—one by one—the minutes that were left.

Chapter 17

A Trail of Question Marks

WORTHINGTON AND BOB ANDREWS were getting anxious. They had been sitting in the Rolls-Royce an hour, waiting for Jupiter and Pete to come back, but so far there had been no sign of them. Every five minutes Bob hopped out of the big car to look up Black Canyon. And every ten minutes or so Worthington got out and took a look, too. It was like staring down the throat of a giant snake.

"Master Andrews," Worthington said at last. "I think that I should go after them."

"But you can't leave the car, Worthington," Bob reminded him. "You're not supposed to let it out of your sight."

"Master Jones and Master Crenshaw are more important than an automobile," Worthington said. "I am going to go search for them."

He got out of the Rolls and opened the rear trunk. Bob was right beside him as the chauffeur picked out a big emergency electric lantern.

"I'm coming with you, Worthington," Bob said. "They're my buddies."

"Very well, we shall go together."

Worthington paused to take a heavy hammer out of the trunk, in case he needed a weapon, and then they started up Black Canyon. Because of his leg, Bob had difficulty keeping up with the tall, rangy chauffeur, but Worthington half lifted him around the worst piles of rocks. In almost no time they were at Terror Castle.

They discovered at once that the front door had no knob, and could not be opened from the outside. Then Worthington spotted the loose knob lying on the tiles.

"Obviously the lads did not enter through the door," he said. "We must look for another entrance."

They ranged up and down the front of the place, flashing the light in the windows. Suddenly Bob spotted the mark—a big ?—chalked on a French window which was slightly ajar.

"They must have gone in here!" he yelled, explaining to Worthington about The Three Investigators' secret mark. They pushed the window open and slipped through. Inside, as Worthington flashed his lantern around, they could see they were in an old dining room.

"No telling where the lads went from here," Worthington said, looking disturbed. "There are several doors and none is marked."

Then Bob spotted the big mirror. There was a question mark chalked in the center.

"They could scarcely have walked into a mirror," said Worthington, perplexed. "Still, it bears investigation."

He grasped the frame of the mirror, and to their amazement it swung open like a door. Behind it there was a narrow passage.

"A secret door!" Worthington exclaimed. "The boys must have gone through here, so we must do the same."

Bob was sure he wouldn't have had the nerve to go down that narrow, pitch-dark passage by himself, but Worthington marched directly into it. Bob had no choice but to go along with him. Discovering the First Investigator's mark on the door at the other end, they went through and found themselves in the projection room. Worthington flashed the light around, over the decaying velvet drapes, the ragged seats, the old dust-covered pipe organ. But they could see no sign whatever of Jupiter and Pete.

Then Bob noticed an odd gleam coming from under the seat. He reached down.

"Worthington!" he shouted. "Here's Pete's new flashlight!"

"Master Crenshaw would not simply leave it here," Worthington said. "Something must have happened in this area. Search carefully for indications."

They got down on hands and knees in the aisle between the seats, and Worthington held his light close to the floor. "Look, the dust here has been disturbed over a large area."

He was right. And in the middle of the place where the dust had been stirred up there was a raggedly chalked white question mark.

Worthington seemed upset when he saw the mark, but he did not tell Bob what he was thinking. Rising, he scouted around carefully until he found footprints in the dust, leading around in front of the seats, then behind the rotted movie screen, and through a door in back of it. Beyond the door was a hall. A flight of steps wound down into more pitch blackness. The hall itself, however, went off in a different direction.

As they stood there wondering which way to go— down the stairs or along the hall—Worthington spied a faint question mark on the top step.

"Down the stairs," he said. "Master Jones is very resourceful. He has marked his trail for us."

"But what do you think happened, Worthington?" Bob asked as they trotted down stairs that wound around and around until he felt dizzy.

"We can only guess," Worthington said, stopping briefly to inspect another chalked mark on a landing. "If Master Jones had been walking, he would have placed his mark at eye level on the wall. I am forced to conclude he was being carried, and that he took the opportunity to make the mark when the person, or persons, carrying him set him down to rest. He could probably touch the floor unseen."

"But who would have carried him down into this

cellar?" Bob asked in dismay. "If it is a cellar. It looks more like a dungeon to me."

"It is exactly like a dungeon I once saw in an old English castle where I was employed," Worthington told him. "A very unpleasant place. As for who may have been carrying Master Jones, I cannot guess. Unfortunately we seem to have lost the trail."

They had reached the bottom. Three different corridors led off in three different directions, each one blacker than the others. And there weren't any more chalk marks.

"Let us turn out the light and listen," the chauffeur said. "In the darkness we may hear something."

They strained their ears in the silent blackness, smelling the damp, musty air. Then, unexpectedly, they heard a sound like a rock scraping against another rock. A moment later they saw a glimmer of light, coming from far down the middle corridor.

"Master Jones!" Worthington shouted. "Is that you?"

For a brief second they saw a woman holding a lighted lantern. Then the light vanished and they heard the sound of scraping rocks again. Once more everything was dark and silent.

"After her!" Worthington shouted. He dashed down the corridor, leaving Bob to hobble after him as fast as he could. By the time the boy caught up with the chauffeur, Worthington was pounding on a smooth concrete wall. The passage simply came to a dead end at that point.

"She went through here!" Worthington said. "I'll swear to that. Stout measures are called for." Pulling the heavy hammer out of his belt, he began smashing at the wall. In a moment they both pricked up their ears. One section sounded hollow.

He gave that spot a few hard smashes, and the cement began to crumble. In no time he had knocked a hole right through the wall. It was only about six inches thick there, made of cement on a wire frame. A secret door! When he found that he could get a hold on the door, Worthington began to yank it back and forth. On the fourth yank it came open, revealing another secret passage behind it. This one seemed to lead directly into the hillside. The roof and sides were formed completely of rock.

"A tunnel!" Worthington exclaimed. "Whoever captured the lads departed through this tunnel. That woman must be one of them. Quick—before she gets away from us."

He tucked Bob under his arm to make better speed and started into the tunnel. After a few feet, the passage became very rough, and the roof dipped down so low that Worthington had to stoop to get through. As he was stooping, he knocked his lantern against the wall and dropped it. The light went out. While Bob was feeling around for the lantern, he heard a flapping of wings all around them, then excited squeaks and chirps. The next moment something soft slammed into him in the darkness. Then another object and another flapped against his head.

"Bats!" Bob yelled in alarm. "Worthington, we're being attacked by giant bats!"

"Steady, lad!" Worthington said. "Don't panic."

He got down on his knees to hunt around for his light, while Bob covered his head with his arms. Large, soft creatures were flapping all around him now, and one tried to light on his head. He gave a wild yell and knocked it off.

"Worthington!" he shouted. "They're big as pigeons! They're giant vampire bats!"

"I think not, Master Andrews," Worthington said as his light finally came on again. He aimed its beam upward, and they could see dozens of things with wings flying around them. But the things were birds, not bats. As soon as they saw the light, they flew toward it, squeaking and screeching in their excitement.

Worthington snapped off the lantern.

"The light attracts them," he shouted to Bob. "We'll make our way back in the darkness. Here, give me your hand."

Bob grasped Worthington's hand, and the Englishman led the way back, groping along the rough wall. The birds seemed to disappear. At least in the darkness they quieted down again, so that the two investigators got to the door and back into the cellar of Terror Castle without any more interference. They closed the door to keep out the birds.

"I don't think the lads were taken through that tunnel," Worthington remarked. "Their captors would have had to put them down to open the hidden door. Then Master Jones would have had a chance to leave a mark. And there is no mark here."

There was no mark. But suddenly a voice started yelling. And there was no mistaking whose voice it was. Jupiter was calling for help. A moment later Pete joined in.

Their voices were coming from in back of Bob and Worthington, and were very muffled. The tall chauffeur hurried back up the dark corridor, and found a closed door he had missed while chasing after the vanishing woman. Inside was a real dungeon cell with iron ring-bolts on the wall. And there were Pete and Jupiter, tied up like Christmas packages. They didn't seem any too happy to be rescued, either. In fact they were annoyed that their yelling hadn't been heard sooner.

As he cut them loose, Worthington explained that in chasing after the mysterious woman and hammering on the hidden tunnel door, he had made too much noise to hear their shouting.

"We must get out of here at once and fetch the authorities," the English chauffeur said, while Jupiter and Pete were dusting themselves off. "These people are dangerous. They left you here to die."

But Jupiter wasn't paying much attention. He had pricked up his ears when Bob mentioned being attacked by birds in the tunnel.

"What kind of birds were they?" he asked.

"What kind of birds?" Bob yelled belligerently. "I didn't stop to ask them. They acted like small eagles, the way they came after us."

"Actually they were harmless," Worthington said. "They were merely attracted by the light. They seemed to be parakeets, Master Jones."

"Parakeets!" The First Investigator acted as if he had been stung by a hornet. "Come on, follow me! We must act fast!"

And getting the flashlight loose from his belt, he dashed out.

"What bit *him?*" Pete asked as Bob handed him his flash.

"A clue, I guess," Bob answered. "Anyway we can't let him go alone."

"Definitely not," Worthington agreed. "We must follow him, lads."

They raced after Jupiter, who was already fifty yards ahead of them, despite his taped ankle. Pete outdistanced Worthington, who paused to assist Bob. As the latter two ducked into the tunnel, they could see the others' lights bobbing along ahead of them—going up, then down, then around a corner of the natural rock tunnel.

They made the best time they could, ignoring the frightened parakeets that fluttered around them. In some spots Worthington had to duck low to squeeze through. Finally they came to a straight section of tunnel, and saw the bobbing lights ahead come to a halt. They hurried along the final stretch and found a wooden door wide open. Stepping through it, they joined Jupiter and Pete in a big wire cage, surrounded by fluttering parakeets screeching in fright.

"We're inside the big cage where Mr. Rex raises his parakeets!" Jupiter yelled to them. "The end of Black Canyon must lie exactly parallel to the end of Winding Valley Road, with only a few hundred feet of rocky ridge separating them. I never thought of that possibility—they start so many miles apart on opposite sides of the mountain."

Jupiter pushed hard on the wire door that closed the cage, and it burst open. All four squeezed out and found themselves just a few feet away from Mr. Rex's little bungalow. Through the window they could see Mr. Rex and a small man with bushy hair playing cards, as if they didn't have a care in the world.

"We'll surprise them," Jupiter whispered. "Extinguish all lights."

They did, and followed him silently around to the front door. He pressed the doorbell. In a moment the door opened. Mr. Rex stood in the doorway, glowering at them. For the first time Bob had an opportunity to see at first hand how sinister he looked, with his bald head and the awful scar on his throat.

"Well, what is it?" Rex whispered in a menacing way.

"We'd like to talk to you, Mr. Rex," Jupiter said.

"And supposing I do not wish to be bothered, boy?"

"In that case"—it was Worthington speaking up—"we shall have to call the authorities to investigate."

Mr. Rex looked alarmed. "No need for that!" he whispered. "Come in, come in."

All four followed him into the room where the other man sat at the card table. He was a very small man, scarcely more than five feet tall.

"This is my old friend, Charles Grant," Rex said. "Charlie, these are the boys who have been investigating Terror Castle. Well, boys, have you found the ghosts yet?"

"Yes," Jupiter said boldly. "We have solved the secret of the castle." He sounded so convinced that he startled both Pete and Bob. If they had solved anything, nobody had told them about it.

"Indeed?" The Whisperer said. "And what is the secret?"

"You two men," Jupiter said, "are the ghosts who have been haunting the castle and scaring people away. And just a few minutes ago you tied up Pete Crenshaw and me and left us in the dungeon under the castle."

The Whisperer scowled at him so hard that Worthington tightened his grip on the hammer.

"That's a very serious accusation, boy," Rex whispered. "And I'll wager you can't prove it."

Which was what Pete was thinking, too. Had Jupe gone off the rails? They had been tied up by an Englishwoman and an old gypsy.

"Look at the tips of your shoes," Jupiter said. "I marked them with our secret mark while you were standing beside me, tying me up."

The two men looked down at their shoes. So did the others.

On the polished black leather of each right toe was chalked the trademark of The Three Investigators—a question mark.

Chapter 18

Interview with a Ghost

BOTH MEN LOOKED startled, as did Pete, Bob and Worthington.

"But——" Pete started to say.

"They were just wearing women's clothes and wigs," Jupiter said. "I realized that when I felt their shoes and discovered they were wearing men's shoes. Then I understood that all five of the gang who captured us were really just two men in different costumes."

"You mean the two Arabs and the Oriental and the two women—they were all Mr. Rex and Mr. Grant?" Pete demanded, dumbfounded.

"He's right." Mr. Rex sounded very weary. "We were acting the part of a large gang to give you boys a real scare. The costumes with robes or skirts we could put on and take off very swiftly. However, I don't want you to think we actually intended to harm you. I was on my way back to untie you when your friends caught sight of me."

"We're not murderers," the little man—Mr. Grant —said. "Nor smugglers either. We're just ghosts."

He chuckled, but Mr. Rex looked solemn.

"I'm a murderer," he said. "I killed Stephen Terrill."

"Oh, that's right." The little man said that as if it was just something that had slipped his mind—like forgetting to wind his watch. "You did do away with *him,* but that hardly counts."

"The police may think differently," Worthington said. "Lads, I think we had better go summon the authorities."

"No, wait." The Whisperer held up his hand. "Give me a moment and I'll let you talk to Stephen Terrill himself."

"You mean talk to his ghost?" Pete yelled.

"Exactly. Talk to his ghost. He will explain to you why I killed him."

Before anybody could do anything to stop him, The Whisperer slipped through a door into the next room.

"Don't worry," Mr. Grant said. "He's not trying to escape. He won't be a minute. By the way, here is your knife back, Jupiter Jones."

"Thank you," Jupiter said. He was attached to that knife.

It was barely sixty seconds before the door opened again, and a man came out. But this time it wasn't The Whisperer. This man was shorter and younger-looking, and had neatly combed gray-brown hair. He wore a tweed jacket and looked at them with a pleasant smile.

"Good evening," he said. "I am Stephen Terrill. You wanted to see me?"

They all stared at him, not knowing what to say. Even Jupiter was silent for once.

Finally Mr. Grant spoke up. "It really is Stephen Terrill," he said.

And then Jupiter looked as if he had bitten into a nice, juicy apple and found half a worm left in it. He looked angry—at himself.

"Mr. Terrill," he said. "You are also Jonathan Rex, The Whisperer, are you not?"

"*Him* The Whisperer?" Pete exclaimed. "Why, he's not as tall, and he's got his hair, and——"

"At your service," said Stephen Terrill. He suddenly whipped off a wig and showed a bald head underneath. He stood very straight, making himself look much taller, squinted his eyes, changed the set of his lips, and hissed: "Stand still! If you value your lives!"

It was so convincing they all jumped. He was The Whisperer, all right. And he was also the movie star who had supposedly died so long ago. That much, at least, Bob and Pete were able to figure out.

Mr. Terrill took from his pocket a curious object. It was an artificial scar, made of plastic.

"When I attached this to my throat, took off my wig and put on elevator shoes, I stopped being Stephen Terrill," he explained. "I reduced my voice to a sinister whisper and became that frightening individual known as The Whisperer."

He put his wig back on and looked like an ordinary man again.

They all started to ask questions at once, and he held up his hand.

"We'd better all sit down," he said, "and I'll explain. You see that picture?" He pointed to the photograph on the table, which showed him shaking hands with The Whisperer—shaking hands with himself, really.

"That was trick photography, of course—to further the illusion of two totally different men. You see, many years ago when I became a moving-picture star, I found my shyness and my lisp made it very difficult to handle my business affairs properly. I hated to talk to people. I couldn't argue for my rights.

"So I created the character of The Whisperer to be my business manager. The Whisperer always whispered in a fierce tone, which hid my lisp; and he looked so menacing that I had no difficulty in dealing with any-one. No one, except my friend Charlie Grant here, knew that I was both men. Charlie was my make-up man, and he used to help me change from being Stephen Terrill into being The Whisperer.

"This scheme worked well until I made my first talk-ing picture. Then the whole world laughed at me! It was a terrible blow to my pride. I withdrew to my home. When I learned the bank wanted to take that away from me too, I became despondent and desperate.

"At the time of building my castle, the workmen had discovered a fault in the rocks of Black Canyon. The fault ran all the way through the ridge to the other side, where Winding Valley Road ended. I had the natural tunnel walled up, but secretly installed a hidden door. Then, as Jonathan Rex, I bought the land at the other end of the secret passage and built a small home there. That way I could come and go and no one would suspect my double identity.

"Often in those days I went for long, solitary drives in an effort to shake off my deep depression. One day I was driving high above the ocean when I conceived the brilliant idea of a faked accident."

"You drove your car off that cliff yourself, didn't you?" Jupiter broke in.

Terrill nodded. "Yes. First I wrote the note, leaving it where someone would be sure to find it. Then one dark, stormy night I staged the accident, letting my car topple over the cliff—without me in it, of course. And that was the end of Stephen Terrill as far as the world was concerned. Also as far as I was concerned. To me he was as good as dead and buried, and I wanted to keep it that way. I also wanted to keep my castle. The thought of anyone else owning it or living in it was too much to bear.

"Although the castle was empty now, I could enter it at will through the natural tunnel. So I was secretly on hand when the police conducted their search, and I made sure they all left in a hurry. When I built the castle, you see, I installed various devices in it for giving my friends thrills. Later these were most useful in helping me to build the public impression that the castle was haunted.

"I made even more of a ghostly disturbance when the bank sent their men to collect my goods. Soon it was scarcely necessary to do anything to frighten those who entered the castle. Their own imaginations did it for them. But I made certain that the fearsome reputation of the building did not wane. And just to make the whole spot seem less desirable to anyone who might even think of buying it, I occasionally rolled rocks down the hillside onto the road.

"My scheme worked. No one wanted to buy the castle from the bank. Meanwhile I began to save money to buy it myself. As Jonathan Rex, a breeder of rare pet birds, I acquired almost enough money for a down payment. . . . Then you boys came along."

The actor sighed.

"You boys were much more stubborn than anyone else had ever been," he said.

"Mr. Terrill," asked Jupiter, who had been listening intently, "did you phone us after our first visit, and use a spooky voice to scare us?"

The man nodded. "I thought it would help keep you away."

"But how did you know we were coming that night, and how did you know who we were?" Jupiter asked.

The actor smiled slightly.

"My friend here, Charlie Grant, is my lookout," he said. The very short man nodded. "Just at the entrance to Black Canyon there is a small bungalow, barely visible. Charlie lives there. Whenever he sees anyone enter the canyon, he telephones me and I hurry through the tunnel to be ready for them.

"When he saw the Rolls-Royce go up the canyon, I recognized it from his description as being the car I had read about in the paper. And of course I had also read that you were the one who had won the use of it.

"You boys left rather hurriedly that night. Please don't feel badly about that—others have left even more swiftly. I returned to my bungalow and looked for your name in the telephone book. Not finding it there, I called Information and found you did have a telephone. So I called you."

"Oh," Jupiter said, and Pete scratched his head. As Jupiter had said, answers to mysteries can be simple—when you know them. But until you know them they can seem plenty tough.

"Then that's why Skinny Norris—that is, those other two boys—left in such a hurry the day Pete and I came to see you," Jupiter remarked.

"Yes, Charlie had warned me and I was waiting for them. However, your arrival at almost the same time caught us unprepared."

Little Mr. Grant looked embarrassed.

"I'd like to explain about that, boys," he said. "When you drove up, it was too late for me to warn my friend Steve. So I slipped into the canyon by a side trail to keep watch. I saw those other boys run out, and watched you chase them. Then I accidentally started a rock rolling, and you looked up and spotted me."

"So it was you we were trying to catch!" Pete exploded. "And you sent that rock slide down on us."

"It was truly an accident," Mr. Grant said earnestly. "The rocks were piled there to push down on the road sometime when they might help discourage a prospective buyer. I tried to hide behind them and dislodged them. I was extremely worried that you had been seriously hurt, though I saw you duck into that rocky crevice. Then I saw the end of a stick appear through the dirt blocking the entrance . . . and I deduced you were safe.

"I waited there until you were safely out, however. If you had encountered difficulty, I would have come to your aid."

At this point Pete couldn't think of anything more to say. At least Mr. Terrill's and Mr. Grant's explanations had cleared up several mysteries. It was easy now to see how the two men had managed to be ready for them every time any of The Three Investigators had visited the castle.

Jupiter was still scowling.

"I believe I understand most of what happened," he said. "But a few points still remain unclear."

"Ask anything you want to," the actor encouraged him. "You've earned the right to know the answers."

"The afternoon we called on you, Mr. Terrill," Jupiter said, "you had a pitcher of lemonade freshly made, as if you were expecting us. You also said you'd been cutting dry brush, and that wasn't true. They are small points, but I'd like to clear them up."

The actor chuckled slightly. "After you escaped from the cave," he said, "you were too preoccupied to see my friend Charlie shadowing you back to the car. He was hidden close enough to hear you give the chauffeur my address. As soon as you drove off he telephoned me.

"I immediately got ready for you. From my window I can see down into a stretch of Winding Valley Road. That antique Rolls-Royce with its gold trimming is a car very easily recognized. As soon as I saw it, I made the lemonade, then slipped out into the bushes, carrying the machete as an excuse. I was watching you as you came up my path.

"At that point I had not decided just how to handle you. I finally decided to be friendly, give you a cold drink, and try to impress you with the frightening quality of Terror Castle so you would stay away of your own accord. Please remember that I did my best to tell you as few untruths as possible. Of course I said that Stephen Terrill was dead—but so he was, in my mind.

"I also said I had never entered the door of the castle again. I never have. I've gone and come through the tunnel. Having the entrance inside my cage of birds, I've been able to slip in and out without ever being noticed. Tonight I was in such a hurry I left the door open, and the birds got into the tunnel.

Jupiter was pinching his lip again.

"The gypsy warning you sent us, Mr. Terrill," he said. "That was your friend Mr. Grant dressed up as an old gypsy woman, was it not?"

"Exactly, my boy. When I learned you three were investigators, I knew you might be persistent. So Charlie made up as a gypsy woman and brought you the second warning. I did hope it would scare you into staying away."

"It actually made me curious, Mr. Terrill," Jupiter said politely. "No one else ever had any warnings. I wondered why we were getting them. Ghosts don't bother to warn people. So I deduced someone human didn't want us around Terror Castle.

"Then, when I studied the photographs Bob made, I noticed that the suit of armor in Echo Hall wasn't very rusty and there wasn't much dust in your library. After so many years, there should have been lots of rust and dust. It certainly looked as if someone was secretly taking care of things in Terror Castle.

"And the person the castle meant most to was the owner, Stephen Terrill. So I deduced at last that you were still alive, sir. Of course, you threw me off the track tonight by acting the role of a gang of international smugglers when you captured us. I believe you were an Arab, the Oriental and the Englishwoman, and Mr. Grant was an Arab and the old gypsy?"

"That is correct." Stephen Terrill's eyes twinkled. "We used part of my large collection of wigs and costumes. I wanted to give you a lasting scare. I thought that if you were worried about the vengeance of a gang of smugglers, instead of mere ghosts, you might abandon your investigation of Terror Castle. You were really becoming much too persistent!

"Well, that just about gives you the whole story. Is there anything else you'd like to know?"

"There's plenty!" Pete piped up now. "For one thing, what about that eye that looked at us from the picture the first night?"

"That was my eye," Stephen Terrill said. "There's a secret passage behind the paintings, and there was a peephole in the picture."

"But when Bob and I examined the picture later on," Pete argued, "there wasn't any hole in it."

"After you fled, I hung another similar picture there," Mr. Terrill said. "Just in case you came back to examine it."

"But the Blue Phantom?" Pete asked. "And the old organ playing that weird music? And the Fog of Fear? And the ghost in the mirror? And the cold draft in the Hall of Echoes?"

"I hate to tell you," the actor said. "It's like a magician telling how he performs his tricks. It takes the mystery away from them. But you've earned the right to know, and if you really want to——"

"I believe I have been able to deduce some of the methods you used, sir," Jupiter said. "The cold draft was a flow of gas from melting dry ice coming through a hole in the wall. The weird music was a record played backwards through an amplifier. The Blue Phantom was probably cheesecloth covered with luminous paint. The Fog of Fear was no doubt some chemical that makes smoke, forced into the secret passage through small holes."

"You're right, boy," Stephen Terrill admitted. "I suppose that once you realized a human agency was behind the strange manifestations, you were able to deduce the method of creating the effects."

"Yes, sir," Jupiter told him. "And the ghost in the mirror was probably a projection of some kind. But one thing I'm not sure of. How did you manage to induce the feeling of nervousness and terror inside the castle?"

"Please don't ask me to tell you everything," the actor begged. "I'd like to preserve some of my secrets. As it is, you've found out enough to ruin all my plans. . . . I want to show you something. Look!"

He flung open the door through which he had ducked to change himself from the sinister Whisperer into Stephen Terrill. Within they saw a large dressing room. There were costumes of every kind hanging from the wall. Wigs were piled high on wig stands. And in one corner was an enormous pile of the sort of round cans used for storing motion picture film.

"There, in that room," the actor said, ". . . *there* is the real Stephen Terrill. Those costumes. Those wigs. All those motion pictures stored in the cans. Those are the real me. Stephen Terrill is just an instrument that transformed those costumes and wigs into strange characters to provide enjoyable thrills for millions of people all over the world.

"For many years Terror Castle was my last pride. There I was still frightening people instead of being laughed at. And all the time I was practicing. I cured my lisp. I managed to speak with a deeper voice. I learned to sound like a ghost, a woman, a pirate, an Arab, a Chinese—dozens of others. I dreamed of making a comeback.

"But as those years passed, the kind of motion picture I made was no longer desired. Now scary pictures are often produced just to get people to laugh. Old pictures shown on television have funny voices and sounds added to produce laughter. And I refuse to degrade my talents to provide cheap laughter!"

Mr. Terrill was becoming quite excited. He slapped his fist into his palm and was breathing hard. "But now there's nothing left for me. I can't be the Phantom of Terror Castle any more. I'll lose the castle itself. I can't be The Whisperer. I don't know what I'll do."

He paused to get control of himself and Jupiter, who had been pinching his lip practically off, spoke again.

"Mr. Terrill," he asked, "do those cans in there contain all of the wonderful scary films you made, which no one has seen for many years?"

The actor nodded, looking at him.

"What are you thinking of?" he asked.

"I have an idea how you can get your castle back and still go on entertaining people by scaring them," Jupiter said. "You see——"

And, as usual, Jupiter had hit upon an incredibly good idea.

Chapter 19

Mr. Hitchcock Makes a Bargain

THE NEXT MORNING, as Worthington and the Rolls whisked them into Hollywood to see Mr. Hitchcock, Jupiter didn't look happy. Pete knew what the trouble was. Jupe was still sore at himself for not deducing that The Whisperer and Stephen Terrill were the same person.

The two boys were visiting Mr. Hitchcock without Bob, who unfortunately had to work that morning.

"As soon as Worthington mentioned that the secret tunnel under Terror Castle was full of parakeets," Jupiter said, coming out of his deep meditation, "I realized that they must be Mr. Rex's—that, in fact, the tunnel must end inside the cage where he raised his birds. And he had accidentally left the entrance open. But I still didn't realize that Mr. Rex was really Mr. Terrill."

"You had everything else figured out," Pete told him. "Even to the fact that Mr. Terrill was still alive, though for a time you got thrown off the track. You ought to be proud of yourself."

But Jupiter just shook his head.

This time, there was no trouble getting in to Mr. Hitchcock. The guard at the gate waved them through, and in a few moments they were seated in the famous director's office.

"Well, lads," Mr. Hitchcock rumbled. "What have you to report?"

"We found a haunted house, sir," Jupiter said.

"Ah, indeed?" The director raised a quizzical eyebrow. "And what type of ghost is it haunted by?"

"That's the trouble," Jupiter confessed. "It's been haunted by a man who is alive, not dead."

"Mmm. That sounds interesting." Mr. Hitchcock settled back in his chair. "Tell me about it."

He listened attentively to the tale. When Jupiter had finished, he remarked, "I'm glad to know that Stephen Terrill is alive. He was a great artist in his day. But I confess I am curious to know how he produced the atmosphere of terror which filled his castle and affected everyone who entered."

"He said he would rather not tell us, sir," Jupiter answered. "But I believe I can make a guess. I was studying a book in order to help my uncle assemble a pipe organ he had bought, and I came across a mention of the fact that subsonic vibrations—too deep and low to be heard—have curious effects on the human nervous system.

"It is my guess, sir, that among the pipes of Mr. Terrill's supposedly ruined pipe organ are several which emit these deep vibrations felt by the body's nervous system, rather than heard. At a distance the effect of the vibrations would be to make one nervous. Close up, a feeling of anxiety and terror would probably result. But naturally the effect would not extend outside the castle, a fact which my partners tested for me one evening."

Pete shot his stocky partner a glance. So that was why Jupe had insisted that he and Bob visit Terror Castle that day! Pete was about to say something scathing, but Mr. Hitchcock started to speak again.

"Young man," he said, "you apparently did a good job of ferreting out the secret of Terror Castle. But now that you have done so, what is to become of Steve Terrill? It does not seem to me you have done him any favor by uncovering his secret."

Jupiter squirmed a little.

"Mr. Terrill has an idea, sir," he said. "In fact, he seems very enthusiastic about it. He is going to the bank with the money he has saved raising parakeets, and arrange to buy back the castle. He has a plan, and I am sure they will lend him more money when he explains it.

"You see, first he will reappear as Stephen Terrill,

the long-lost movie star, and move back into the castle. There will be many stories in the newspapers, naturally."

"Naturally," Mr. Hitchcock agreed, eyeing Jupiter down his nose. "And then what?"

"Next he will open his castle to the public for an admission fee. He will show his famous old scary pictures in his private projection room. He will also let people wander around the castle, which will remain almost exactly as it is now. Tourists will go there in great numbers to enjoy the films and to be frightened by the Fog of Fear and other devices Mr. Terrill has installed in the castle for giving people a harmless thrill.

"Mr. Terrill will also demonstrate, in various costumes, his portrayal of the sinister figures he played in his greatest movies. I am sure it will be a great success."

"Hmmm." Alfred Hitchcock studied the stocky lad. "I suspect, young Jones, that I detect your active young imagination in the plan you have just set forth. But let that pass. The Three Investigators have done a commendable job, even though you were unable to find me a house haunted by genuine ghosts. I will stand by my word and introduce your account of the case when it is written."

"Thank you, sir," Jupiter said. "It will mean a lot to The Three Investigators."

"If it is any consolation," Mr. Hitchcock said, "the difficulty of finding a genuine haunted house proved so great that I have abandoned that particular project. But tell me, what are your plans now?"

Pete was tempted to speak up and say their plans were for a little peace and quiet, getting over some of the harrowing moments that Terror Castle had provided. But Jupiter spoke first.

"We are investigators, Mr. Hitchcock. We will start looking for another case at once."

The director eyed him shrewdly.

"I don't suppose you're planning to come back and ask me to introduce your second case, when you get one, are you?" he demanded.

"No, sir," Jupiter said with dignity. "I had no such idea in mind. However, if you would be willing to do so——"

"Not so fast, young man!" Mr. Hitchcock thundered, and Jupiter subsided. "I said nothing of the sort. Nothing whatever of the sort."

"No, sir," Jupiter said meekly.

The director glowered at him for a moment, then continued.

"I had in mind," he said at last, "to suggest a case for you. An old friend of mine, a former Shakespearian actor, has lost his parrot. He was very much attached to the parrot. The police apparently are of no help. You have shown—I must confess it—a certain ingenuity. Perhaps you can help him find his parrot. Unless"—he gave Jupiter and Pete a frown— "hunting for lost parrots is too tame a task for The Three Investigators."

"No, sir!" It was Pete who spoke this time. If they had to go on a case, hunting for a lost parrot sounded to him like just about as much excitement as he cared for at the moment. "Our motto is, 'We investigate anything.'"

"We will be glad to try to help your friend, sir," Jupiter said.

Mr. Hitchcock smiled. It was a smile that might be hiding certain secret thoughts, but they could not be certain.

"In that case," he said, "I will also introduce this case for you."

"Thank you, sir!" the boys said in unison.

"But only on one condition!" the director stated firmly. "It has to be a case worth writing about. Obviously, simply finding a lost parrot, even if it is a parrot that stutters, is not enough to warrant writing a book about. If the case turns out to be a simple and easy one, naturally I shall have nothing further to do with it or with The Three Investigators."

"Did you say the parrot *stuttered?*" Jupiter asked, his eyes already alight with interest.

"I did," the man stated. "Did you also hear what else I said?"

"Yes, sir!" Jupiter replied. "I never heard of a stuttering parrot before. Come on, Pete, we've got our second case!"

"One moment!" Mr. Hitchcock said, and they paused. "I believe it would help if you had my friend's name and address." He wrote something on a sheet of paper. "Here it is."

"Thank you," Jupiter said. He tucked the paper into his pocket, then started toward the door with Pete. "We'll let you know how we make out, sir," he said, just before they left.

Mr. Hitchcock watched them go with a slight smile. Quite a story, he thought—"The Secret of Terror Castle."